DAFFODIL

DAFFODIL

An existential odyssey
through space, time,
and a young woman's mind.

Truant D. Memphis

To all the lost souls. Someday we will find you.

*Special thank you to Nathan Miller, Esq.
for his reporting on the Rohm-Bridicata trial.*

*Special thank you to Jessi You Know Who You Are
for use of the eyes and brains.*

FOREWORD

This history was originally recorded over a decade ago in my current chronological line, during much simpler times. Ahem. Cough.

While I remain equally as confused today, I was much angrier then. Praise Bob, praise Bob.

—T.M.

DISCLAIMER

No children were harmed in the making of this book. They were harmed long before it was written.

Well, okay, maybe at the same time. That sort of depends on how you perceive existence.

Either way, they weren't harmed by me.

Section I

MISSION ASSIGNMENT: 514
SOUL TRANSMISSION: ALPHA
ACTIVE UNIT: 257-A
RECORDING TECHNICIAN: AO41

Following multiple host initiated aborts, I have successfully entered a human womb. Genetic analysis indicates my body will be female. Barring unforeseen gestation complications, mission assignment 514 is Go status.

Due to species evolutionary limits, this will be the only pre-mission or inter-mission report, with Omega Transmission to follow upon assignment completion.

Assignment pretext is suspension time for the Rohm-Bridicata incident. 257-A is serving suspension as a low level Rotation Unit until the trial resumes. This is my fifth successive assignment serving suspension time, my first on Earth. The trial has been on continuance for 30 Rohmian years and 125 Bridicatan years. Though irrelevant to the trial or my suspension assignment, in relative time cycles, the Rohm-Bridicata trial has been on continuance for about 1,635 Earth years. I will note for the record, once again, the Rohm-Bridicata incident was beyond any agent's ability to prevent.

Anomaly report: While traversing organic hosts to facilitate my assignment to Earth, during formless interdimensional stasis, I was intercepted by Agent 13. I am now in possession of an unidentified archaic Macrocosm. If received by any of the previous hosts to which I was submitted, I would not have encountered Agent 13. Requesting a reprieve for the following unapproved break in transmission formality: I cannot explain in detail the fortuitous nature of my encounter with Agent 13. Please ensure that statement is duly noted in the final report. I have something very special. If Agent 13 and I had not intersected, we might all already be dead. I do not mean moved around, I mean infinitely dead. It is my conclusion my suspension assignment has been updated with additional parameters.

I am entering the final phases of Human gestation. Memory suppression and disconnection from telepathic transference channels have initiated. 257-A signing off for lifecycle inception. Monitor my trip closely. Praise Bob.

I

My name is Truant Memphis. This story is about my beloved. She's the only person I've ever known who made breathing an art form. She was born crazy in the most beautiful way, and she stole my soul the moment we met. I was sixteen. She is the only one, ever. Do you get it yet? Good. Her name is Daffodil Fields.

The first time I saw Daffodil was in the year 3023. We were in the future, I think. I'm not certain what day today is. Look at a clock. Whatever that lying fucker says is close enough.

Daffodil is my wife. Not in the eyes of the laws of any land, but in the eyes of all that matters to a man. Our wedding ceremony was presided over by a creature with wings who lives in a floating city disguised as a cloud. That was pretty cool. Daffodil and I have a daughter named Peaceful Dreaming Memphis, Sweet Pea for short. An angel born with two twinkles in her eyes. One says, "I can't stay for long. I really like it here, but I must be moving along." The other is all the places in her head she might like to visit. They're places you and I can only dream of, but unlike us, when she dreams them somewhere they become real (…another story, another day…).

We have a son named Daniel Trate. Our little fighter, destined for greatness and cosmic nonsense. I knew a few of Daniel's ancestors. He comes from a long line of honorable men. When we found him, Daniel was an orphan, just like Daffodil and me. Now we all belong to each other, but the story of us is for another day. This is for Daffodil.

She was born in Indiana to parents who were "mentals." That's what we often called crazy people when I was a kid, mentals. Daffodil's folks were flower children of the nineteen-sixties, much like my own parents, except hers were a little over watered. Their root structure got damaged and they had to be isolated from the rest of the garden. In other words, they ate a bunch of drugs and lost their minds. There is something slightly beautiful about the whole deal, I suppose. They were in love, and wherever their minds went I'm pretty sure they went together.

"Nine, one, one. How can we help?" The dispatcher's voice was familiar to the supermarket's manager.

"Anna, it's Lou again. I've got two youngsters in the store that appear to be on drugs or something."

"Are they causing trouble? Is the situation violent?"

"No, no. They just seem lost. They're holding hands and wandering around aimlessly. They aren't looking at anything to buy and their eyes are glazed. Vacant. I think it's drugs. I'm not calling to get them in trouble or anything. Just trying to get them some help."

"Alright. I'll send someone over."

When the police arrived they took a homeless man and pregnant young homeless woman into custody. Within hours the couple was hospitalized and locked up tight. Daffodil was born shortly after. In an apparent moment of clarity during the birth, her mother grabbed an attending nurse and repeated the word daffodil over and over. The nurse, seeing the last name Fields, thought Daffodil seemed an appropriate name for the child. And pretty. That nurse was part of the pediatric wing, not the twelfth floor where all the crazies lived. She didn't realize daffodil was the only word the young, insane mother had managed to utter intelligibly during her stay in the psych ward.

At birth, by all physical appearances, Daffodil had escaped the folly of her parents. All twenty digits, two ears, two eyes, etc.

"Doctor the baby appears fine physically, but she isn't behaving normal." This was a nurse, a few weeks after Daffodil was born.

"Anything specific you're concerned with?"

"Well, I don't think she's cried once. You can see her eyes constantly moving when closed, and when they're open they aren't responsive to stimulus."

"Odd. Let's do some blood work and a CT scan."

The eventual diagnosis was schizophrenia. Daffodil's brain showed neurocognitive anomalies commonly found in adult sufferers of the disorder. Schizophrenia is a much broader subject than one might realize, and does not always lead to craziness – at least, not the kind of crazy that puts your name in the papers and frightens people. Some believe Albert Einstein may have been mildly schizophrenic, lending to his genius. Basically, we really don't seem to know a lot about our brains from what I've read. Even less from what I've seen. Perhaps the better commentary is, despite all we think we know about the brain, there is a shit-ton more we don't.

And yes, I just made "shit-ton" a scientific measure. Seriously, your children will learn it in school. I can do stuff like that. My contract with the universe is a lengthy document.

Back to Daffodil. The doctors knew her brain was different, so they chose a word to define the anomaly, which in this instance was their way of saying, "We don't have one damn clue what's wrong with this one, but we're pretty sure something is."

Daffodil was made a ward of the state and placed in foster care. Her birth parents were disowned by their own families long before they lost their minds and created her, so Daffodil had no blood relatives in her life. At age five, Daffodil was adopted by her foster family, the Smiths, with whom she'd been living for several years. Daffodil's foster parents were far sicker than her birth parents.

For our children's sake, and my own selfish reasons, I will not describe to you the atrocities Daffodil suffered at the hands of her foster parents. I will simply say that if you can imagine something horrible, it may have happened, and if the particulars did not, an equal level of psychological and emotional torture that would arise from whatever situation you imagined most definitely occurred. Here is a young lady who, by all accounts, was being shit on by the universe.

Daffodil had two best friends growing up. One was a ghost named Tom, who she assumed was the work of her imagination. The other was her brother, Darius. Darius was the same age as Daffodil and the natural born child of Daffodil's adoptive parents. Supposedly, he was autistic.

Growing up in rural Indiana was a stroke of luck in at least one aspect. There weren't many ghosts haunting the woods and corn-fields surrounding Daffodil's home. Tom was the only one she would meet until she left home, and as I mentioned before, she didn't know he was a ghost. As confusing as her childhood already was, this was a blessing.

When Daffodil was six years old she met Tom. She and Darius were in the woods near their home, just outside of French Lick, Indiana. The year was 1982. The siblings were goofing around in a stream when they stumbled upon a pair of bullfrogs they thought would be fun to kidnap. Daffodil imagined the frogs as brother and sister, and could not deny the impulse to add them to her own family. The frogs however, when approached by the two-legged giants, abandoned each other quickly, escaping in opposite directions. "See you on the other side, if you make it," one of the frogs croaked, and that was the end of their partnership.

Daffodil and Darius gave chase, each after their own amphibian doppelganger. It was a poor decision. Before she knew what happened, Daffodil found herself standing in the middle of the creek with a magnificent bullfrog and no brother. She wandered for quite some time with the frog held out in front of her, screaming Darius' name to no avail. Eventually, she did what a child is supposed to do. She sat down and cried. That's when she met Tom.

2

This is important: Time is meaningless here in my little room. In general, the story I'm telling you happened all at once, at the same time, on different planes of chronological existence. But, what I am about to tell you next is what is happening while I'm telling this story, while you're reading this story, until the very end. Unless there is no end, in which case what is happening right now will still be happening. You see, while everything else happens in the past, present and future, what I am about to tell you is happening in all three at the same time. Make sense? Are you with me? Good.

This is important: There are three creatures on the run through a maze of hallways. One looks like a ferret, one looks like a human, and the last looks like evil. One creature has the key to the universe's heart. One is trying to destroy the universe. The other is trying to save it.

The ferret is carrying a sock in its mouth. Inside the sock is a key. The ferret is being chased by a monster-creature-something evil that I'm not ready to describe yet. The human is hunting the monster.

There are other creatures in these hallways as well, searching, hunting, wandering, and arguing. This is a crazy place.

The ferret weaves in and out between legs, feet, stumps, tentacles, and other appendages used to travel the ground. Evil follows close behind, bashing the other creatures out of its way, a bull in a china shop. The human is also close behind. Not so close as to see the ferret, but just close enough to follow the villain's path of destruction.

The hallways are filled with doors through which our three players run in and out. Don't worry about where the doors lead for the time being. Just picture an old cartoon style chase scene with a ferret, a dark skinned noble hero dude, and an evil monster all running in and out of different doors, one chasing the other until it is all happening so quickly that you can't tell who is chasing who. My favorite was Scooby-Doo.

Oh yeah, the monster has wings. They look like the wings of the flying machine Leonardo da Vinci supposedly designed. Powered by a small crank, the wings are barely strong enough to keep the monster afloat from the ground. The crank is mounted chest high on the monster and has a handle on each side. The monster has a second set of arms, very tiny arms that work furiously to spin the crank fast enough for the wings to flap. These wings are temporary. The monster cast a spell on itself so it could fly inside the maze of hallways and doors. The spell didn't quite work out correctly.

The ferret is much swifter than the monster, but as luck would have it, through perpetual motion, sheer will, and dumb luck use of the many doors, the monster manages to stay hot on the ferret's heels. For much the same reasons, excluding of course the really stupid wings, the human stays close behind as well.

One last thing. If you've never seen a ferret run with a sock in its mouth, well, it's absolutely adorable. They arch their back, run halfway sideways, and sort of hop back and forth from their front to back legs. A little, furry war dance. Adorable.

3

"Why are you crying?"

Tom looked down upon Daffodil with genuine empathy, a characteristic that had carried him through most of his physical life. True, there were a few eras of bitterness during his time as a "solid," but for the most part, he never ignored the tears of a fellow creature. Especially a child's. Despite his soothing tone, Tom's voice was a surprise to the distraught little girl. She screamed, full lunged.

"It's okay, it's okay," said Tom, hands held out to his sides.

On instinct, Daffodil tossed her bullfrog – moments before her only consolation for her lost brother – at Tom. Then she jumped up to run, but the frog's strange course stayed her sneakered feet. She watched with amazement as the croaker flew straight through what should have been Tom's chest. Even the frog looked back with surprise, appearing curious as to what he'd just flown through. He wasn't. Bullfrogs can't see ghosts and apparently their faces aren't much for expressions either. Mr. Amphibian Ass was actually giving Daffodil the stink-eye. Stockholm syndrome had not yet infected this angry little guy, and before he hopped away, the frog felt it was important to make his former capture aware of his disdain.

Calm washed over Daffodil when she realized Tom was only make-believe. At this point in her young life her brain was still developing physically, and she'd only been visited a few times by the guests of her subconscious. Each time she considered them her imagination. Though he was a ghost, she regarded Tom the same way.

"You're not real," she said, quietly sniffling and smearing a few tears around her cheeks.

"I'm real enough, if you can see me. Wait, you can see me?"

"Yes."

"You can hear me?"

Daffodil simply nodded her head in response. She was too upset about Darius for this nonsense.

"No one's ever actually heard me before. Or seen me for that matter. At least not recently." Tom stood bewildered. "Have you ever seen a ghost before? Any around here? Jesus, Tom she's a little girl. Can you really hear me?"

"Yes."

"Wow. Weird. This could be really big. I don't know how or why, but this feels big." Tom required a few moments of his own silence to gather his composure. Then he remembered what the whole point was in the first place. "Why are you so upset? And why are you out here all alone? Sometimes the woods can be dangerous you know."

"I'm not alone. I'm with my brother, but he ran away and I can't find him."

This admittance brought forth a fresh wave of salty tears from the little girl, a mixture of fear and failed responsibility. Emotions Tom recognized instantly. That was that. Tom fell in love with the little girl – a parental love mind you – and from that moment forth would spend the rest of his afterlife protecting her.

"Well, what if I help you look for him?" said Tom.

A faint smile creased the corners of the little girl's mouth beneath the dirt and tears.

"Would you like that?"

With a positive nod, Daffodil rose to her feet.

Daffodil and Tom didn't speak as they searched. The girl's eyes remained dry but the prospect of her breaking down into tears again was uncomfortable for Tom. He stayed silent and hoped she would maintain her calm. Though Tom was never the most insightful fellow when alive, time spent as a ghost had broadened those horizons, and for once, his instincts served him well.

The companionship alone had settled the girl enough to get her back on her feet and looking for her brother. So, they quietly searched and Tom continued to study the little lady. There was something different about her. Not the fact she could see him, which is much more frequent in children than most of us choose to remember (although Tom didn't know that, I just thought you should). No, there was something "open" about her. Tom's lack of understanding for his own situation denied him the ability to explain what he was sensing, but he could feel the special nonetheless.

Tom the ghost was the residue of an Indiana high school basketball legend named Thomas Jones. To those who knew, the name Thomas "Bankshot" Jones carried an air of mystery, awe, and sadness. While alive, Tom was hoisted upon the shoulders of men for triumphs on the basketball hardwood. A shooting phenomenon, Tom was the closest thing to Pistol Pete Maravich outside of the Pistol himself, and many years before the Pistol at that.

The name Bankshot was earned after a thirty-six point outing his first year of high school. A member of the varsity squad as a freshman, Tom didn't get much playing time early on, but eight games into the season everything changed. The starting point guard went down with an ankle sprain during the first quarter and that was all she wrote. Sing large woman sing.

Tom hit his first jump-shot seconds into the line-up. When the opposing defender had the audacity to tell him those were the last points he would score, Tom just laughed. "Buddy, I'm gonna score on you whenever I want to for the rest of this game, and I ain't gonna shoot nothing but bank shots." The rest, they say, is history. Tom didn't miss one shot that game, and as promised, each one kissed the backboard on its way through the hoop. I have no idea why Tom wasn't already in the starting line-up if he was that good. If I was forced to speculate, my first guess would be nepotism, one of the most frustrating yet equally understandable practices of any sentient species.

After high school Tom went on to play college ball for his beloved Indiana Hoosiers, living a storied career and fulfilling all the expectations placed upon him, save one. Senior year. There were three seconds left on the clock and two free-throws would give the Hoosiers a one point lead. Bankshot had already scored thirty-two points and now stood at the line with one more chance to give his team a victory. This was the moment he'd been waiting for, pursuing, dreaming about his entire life: The Championship. He was one-hundred percent from the free-throw line the first thirty-nine point fifty-seven seconds of the game. I suppose we know where this is going?

The first shot clanged off the side of the rim, hopeless. The second teased its victim. The ball circled the rim with the malice of a madman before falling away, laughing all the while as it murdered Tom's dream. He sank to his knees and stared at the goal as tears welled in his eyes. That was the first time he died inside, and though it was not the end of his life nor his last embrace with glory and failure, this was a moment that would haunt him forever. Sometimes, when it seems a ghost is haunting your house or your cornfield or your television set, they're really haunting themselves.

Tom was not one of these ghosts, having given up on haunting himself years before we meet him. No, Tom was just lonely. It seemed he'd been forgotten.

You see, being a ghost was not at all what Tom would have imagined, if he had been prone to imaginings when he was alive. Which he wasn't. For the most part, Tom had been a straight-line thinker. To not have a robust imagination made sense for an athlete. At least, it made sense to Tom. An athlete's thought processes are constantly filled with stats, drills, schedules, match-ups, film work, practice, scouting reports, you get the idea. Tangible thoughts. Functional thoughts. Thoughts of constant improvement. However, when you're gifted at something and you do that same thing your entire life, though you may mature at your craft, the emotional transition from child to adult can be affected. Even stunted. For Tom, this *puer aeternus* that being a professional ballplayer afforded him in his days as a flesh-bag lent itself to flights of imaginative fancy in his afterlife. He was, after all, almost completely alone in his hauntings, and if not already truly dead, bored to death.

When Tom had finally given himself over to the concept of being undead, that he was indeed a ghost, he was severely disappointed with his lack of understanding for the situation. There should have been a manual or something. Existence simply isn't fair. Death was just as confusing, lonely, and hurtful as life. Almost as hard as living too, except without the worry for food or clothes, or shelter, or water. What a sham death was.

Yet, this seemingly eternal prison sentence of solitude, coupled with the inability to shoot a basketball, gave Tom the opportunity to follow a new path. In death, he stepped forward on a journey of self-discovery, letting go of all the distractions from his life as a breather. He finally sought understanding for his life, his surroundings, and his place in the universe. He asked himself questions and found his own answers. He spent time alone with his thoughts, allowing them to frighten him, make him sad, make him happy, and comfort him.

Now, although he discovered these new processes, somehow the thought never occurred to him that maybe, just maybe, this self-discovery was why he was still on Earth. If he had paid more attention when he was alive, perhaps just been a little more introspective in general, he might have gone somewhere else when he died. Luckily this thought never burdened him, because the ghost world is often a place of regret, and regret makes an afterlife a complete waste of time. Also, we need Tom. If he'd been more introspective when he was alive, he might have wound up somewhere else in death. Thus, in summation to his back story, if ifs and buts were candy and nuts, Tom would never have met Daffodil, and we would all most likely be dead.

4

This next part is difficult to explain. I will share many of these words with you as they were shared with me, by someone who enjoys speaking in a prophetic manner. Which, by the way, sounds utterly ridiculous when said person is discussing common things, such as using the restroom or having a snack. "In the waning morn, afore the day's burdens hath taketh hold, verily, I did poop. Consequently, rendered faint from exertion, yet not upon the brunching hour, thine humble raconteur did eateth of the candied bar." Or something like that…

Anyways, here we go:

The nature of existence insists on balance in all things. From the beginning, there could be no Nothing without an Everything. Thus, in the days ere all that was, is, and someday might be, from Nothing came Everything. The Lord our Bob awoke, and Bob was Everything.

And whilst Everything did grow, indeed, so too did the emptiness, the Nothing, cosmic ballast to the eternally pitched vessel that is life. Yet, as nature persisted on its irrevocable path to balance, the

Lord Our Bob continued to fill her many universes with the insta-bility of life. As Bob grew existence, filling the cosmos with life and light, her energies often found themselves swimming into the sea of empty. The emptiness however, could not concede. Eventually, in the depths of existence's abyss, within the darkness of the infinite empty, the cosmic excess that was our Lord's good nature and desire to create was transformed. The Nothing that was became a some-thing that would be, and another child was born. A child, destined a warrior, born to defend the Nothing from the onslaught of all things wholesome, all things alive. That warrior is Timmy.

Okay, his name wasn't really Timmy at first, but metaphysical creatures that are actually the embodiment of the existential empti-ness that balance the cosmic scales between existence and nothingness and thereby allow for the existence of existence don't usually have names. Although sometimes they have hundreds. Timmy is one of those sometimes. Timmy is a name from one of his many lives and I chose it for this retelling because childish names frighten me, and because although this is a true story it is mine to tell, so you're stuck with my choices. I promise to painstakingly deliberate over every single decision. I promise.

Timmy, though endowed with seemingly infinite cosmic power, is no Bob. The creature is a byproduct, an end result, a supernatural jerk-kneed reaction to existence's self-imposed house rules. An immortal loner, abandoned to the void of nowhere, defender of the empty space existence insists upon. Yet, Timmy's unjust preordained solitude paved way to insanity's callous embrace. Grandeur became his loveliest delusion, and though not his place, Timmy desired the kingdom of which the Lord our Bob had been blessed to create. The monster welcomed light into the darkness he was designed to protect. Defiled by the darkness, the creations of the displaced light were twisted and broken. A new universe grew without the watchful eye and benevolent hand of a loving creator. Meanwhilst, emptiness found a new space where nothingness persisted, maintaining balance. And Timmy waited. And Evil was born.

Let's recap: There was Nothing. From Nothing came Everything, creating balance. That Everything was God, Allah, Yahweh, the Force, Mother Nature, Gaia, a figment of other peoples' imaginations, whatever the hell you want to call it. I call her Bob. Bob was lonely so she started making stuff. Some of that stuff leaked into dark places that were meant to remain empty. A creature was born to defend these empty spaces from life, maintaining our cosmic balance. That creature, Timmy, went crazy. Timmy quit his defense, flooding the Nothing's natural void with Bob's energy. A broken and twisted universe was created. Meanwhile, somewhere there is still an emptiness, a Nothing, the counterbalance to Everything, which we are all a part of.

Oh for fuck's sake, Bob is God and Timmy's the bad guy.

Scientifically speaking, this story takes place across multiple universes, otherwise known as the multiverse. For the sake of this narrative, once this chapter is over, I refer to the concept of all other universes and Earth's universe as simply, the universe. There is an argument to be made that if humans would stop being so possessive of their little corner of existence, the term multiverse is superfluous, as any and all other existent universes would simply all be a part of one super-universe, which again, is really just saying universe, right? (Don't get me started on how any of the supposed universes outside our own universe might simply be parallel layers of the same universe and most likely sufficiently represented within the category of alternate dimension…) It's that "uni" thing that gets me. The term multiverse feels to me like a game of linguistic scientific footsy, getting fresh with terminology as foreplay for intellectual copulation. Perhaps what we really need, rather than the title multiverse, is a new sub category between universe and galaxy, and scientists who have a lot more sex. Don't waste time trying to decipher my incongruous joke. Just keep in mind that no matter how you organize or label all this nonsense, this organizational chart of the cosmos, it's all Bob.

Anyway, our heroes and villains will be bouncing around all areas and layers of existence, including the delicately woven cosmic tapestry our heroes' journey wads up and tosses in reality's hamper: Time.

Once Timmy was strong enough he ravaged the broken, godless universe he allowed to be born, making it his own. This universe's creatures lived in peril from Timmy's wrath and their own miserably crippled existence, surviving in agony while Timmy fed upon the weariness of their souls. Yet, Timmy was still no Bob, and as his insanity grew, so too did his jealousy of our creator. To the point, Timmy hates us, he hates our existence, and he wants nothing less than the complete destruction of everything that is Bob. Unfortunately, Timmy's figured out how to usher in said annihilation. Fortunately, he's a buffoon.

5

Tom and Daffodil only walked a short while before Daffodil suddenly struck out to the left of the creek bed they followed, exclaiming to Tom she'd found Darius. Another half-hour passed before they could see Darius, but she led Tom straight to him. Tom's only purpose, it appeared, was companionship. Daffodil always found Darius. At age six, she was still too young to recognize this ability, too young to understand that she and her brother were more than just very close friends, too young to realize her autistic brother was psychic and that she herself was something so uniquely powerful there were no words sufficient within themselves with which to label her capabilities. Hence the formation of the necessarily lengthy previous sentence.

When Daffodil and Tom found Darius, he was standing in front of what looked like a small dark cloud. The unidentified floating object hovered a few feet off the ground. Before Daffodil could make sense of the situation, Darius grabbed her by the wrist and headed for home.

Tom had never seen anything like this before. Very few people or ghosts have. The phenomenon might have seemed completely random, an unprecedented occurrence with no explanation whatsoever. A singularity. Frankly, the cloud thing was not. Darius hadn't stumbled upon this strange sight in the woods, he had stumbled through the woods until this strange sight found him.

Three years passed before Daffodil would see the mysterious cloud thing again. By that time she'd forgotten about it and Tom the ghost altogether. Darius had not.

This is important. In Daffodil's ninth year of survival, her brother disappeared. Their father had become upset and assaulted the boy. Wounded, Darius fled the scene. Guess where he went. That's correct.

In effort to protect Darius, Daffodil remained behind to take the beating meant for him. Eventually, she made her escape as well, racing into the woods to find her brother. Instead she found it. The weird looking cloud thing. She'd seen this before, she remembered, and she instantly knew where her brother had gone. Daffodil could feel him in there.

"Hello." The words startled Daffodil. She whirled to see who made them, and there stood Tom the ghost. "Remember me?"

Daffodil nodded her head.

"Is something wrong?"

Again, a silent nod.

"Would you like me to help?"

"No." Daffodil's stare returned to the cloud thingy.

"Are you sure? I'd really like to if I can."

"You can't mister."

Tom opened his mouth to speak again but instead remained silent. Daffodil took a step towards the floating darkness. "I don't think that's a good idea," said Tom.

Daffodil sniffled, tried to fight back her tears, failed, then gave into them, flopping her butt down onto the ground while they had their way. "Where have you been?" she asked Tom, in between sobs.

"In there," he said, motioning towards the mysterious sight in front of her.

"I think my brother's in there now. Is he? Do you know?"

"Yes, he is," Tom said. Then he thought, *One way or another, we all are.*

6

He's thoughtless. Or at least he was, up until right now. (Or then?) He's not certain where he is. Nothing moves. Can't turn his head, can't feel his tongue, and damn well doesn't want to think about what he just thought about.

What do you think it was?

He doesn't know who he is anymore. For that matter, he's not sure he ever did, and he don't mean metaphorically. Nope, he currently has no idea who he is or once was, but I do. His name is Curtis Gout.

What the hell is goin on? (Repeat five times.)

I can't talk, or if I can talk, then I can't hear. My tongue ain't movin. Nothin's movin, dummy. Ya can't talk. But I can see. Why can I see? Can't blink. Can't move my eyes but I can definitely see. That's a ceilin. Yes sir, if I ever seen one.

How'd I get here? (Repeat as necessary.)

And where in Bob's name is here? (Don't waste your time on this one, Curtis. Not right now.)

If he could breath, he would take ten deep breaths. Calm down, Curtis. Let go. First ponder what you know, then consider what may be. You are currently powerless. Your only present faculties are thought and straight-line sight. What else do you know Curtis Gout?

For our dear readers, Curtis, I will tell you, you used to be human. You are human, at the heart of things.

I'm human. Curtis doesn't know why, but he is certain. Otherwise, he has no memory. Not much to work with.

Everyone basically assumes if we have a soul, it's in the heart. It's not. Your soul, if you are so blessed as to have one, is actually in your head, typically behind a locked door dressed with a sign that reads, "Do Not Disturb." Curtis Gout's soul is trapped in a jigsaw puzzle. An unfinished jigsaw puzzle to be exact. The puzzle rests on an old folding table in the parlor of an even older woman.

It's the future. At least, it is from someone's point of view. Has to be. I think.

Curtis doesn't know if he's reading her mind or if the old broad's sharing it with him. *I suppose since I never read no one's mind before, she must be sharin.* Curtis is an excellent guesser. He wonders if she knows he's listening. For that matter, he wonders if she knows she's communicating. You should too.

7

There must be a benevolent king out there somewhere. That's what I was thinking one time, right before I found myself on Shar-Crypt-On. There, I met a fantastic king. He was an enormous king, and a kingly king, and a jolly king, and a wise, handsome king, and a compassionate…okay that's enough. Known forward as The King, this guy was stupendous.

The King of Shar-Crypt-On ruled his planet for thousands of years (though, perhaps only hundreds in respect to your personal timeline). He wasn't just the ruler of his own planet. The King was inter-universal, serving as a member of multiple intergalactic counsels, the president of his space sector's comet watching club, alumni captain of his planet's football team, and Chairman of the Board of Trustees at the University of Universal Reality.

The King met Bob shortly after his Queen passed away. Bob still visits many creatures that exist on planets less cynical than Earth – if he went to Earth today would anyone there believe it was him – and when one of the greatest women in the universe passed away, Bob went to share his condolences and fill The King with new purpose.

Our Lord Bob entrusted The King with a particularly dramatic mission. He must protect the most important key ever created. Most of the time this involves The King forgetting he even has the damn thing, despite his cleverness.

At this very moment, or at least the moment right before this one, or perhaps right after, or at least this very moment in some other plane of existence which might be in the past or future from me and you but is happening currently as far as The King is concerned…

Shoo. Anyway. The King lay in his royal bed, trapped in the high security prison of the mind: a coma.

8

Darius had known somehow the floating thingy would take him away, and he had stepped through with little concern for the "where" portion of the away. When he went into the floating thing he was nine years old. When he came out, his body was still nine years old. His mind was not.

Both his nine-year-old body and his now considerably more mature mind discovered a dark hallway on the other side of the weird cloud thing. A haunted air raised the hair on the back of his neck. The boy whirled around, thinking he might want to jump back through the mysterious cloud and run home, but there was no more cloud. Just an endless hallway and a bunch of doors. He turned around again, this time fully taking in his surroundings. This was the dead end of the dark hallway. One door appeared to be open. A sliver of light poked through the crack into the hallway. Darius shrugged his shoulders, cracked the door a little further, poked his head in, then stepped the rest of the way through. As he stood in wonder, he didn't hear the door shut and lock behind him. Wouldn't have mattered if he did.

Now Darius stared at the most beautiful grass he'd ever seen. I could go on, layering prose with flowery hypothetical descriptions of his appreciation. But, in truth, describing the extent of his appreciation is difficult, as it is hard for me to describe the intricacy of his thought processes. I know Darius loved simple things like grass, and was blessed with the ability to witness obscure beauty, although there was nothing obscure about his new surroundings. Where Darius found himself after he stepped through the doorway, everything he saw was the most beautiful he'd ever seen.

For many weeks he wandered, though always in the same general direction. The weather was perfect everyday. Even when rain showered, it was a lovely, soft, inoffensive, pleasant perfect rain that somehow made him feel healthier and happier. And as soon as the rain came it went. Clouds would instantly dissipate, while the lingering moisture painted the sky with the most picture perfect rainbows you could ever see.

Food made itself known to Darius. No sooner did he think of the possibility he might later become hungry than he would stumble upon the exact thing he craved, when he hadn't yet known what he was craving to begin with! There were fruits and nuts. There were unexplained patches of various vegetables. Most were varieties he'd never before seen. All the edibles he found were delicious, and they kept him more than comfortably fed.

Darius didn't see any other people and didn't think he would. This was a very solid feeling he had. There were many types of animals though, and they were wonderific. Wonderific is a word he created just for describing those animals. You can use it, if you like, when you try to imagine a landscape full of docile alien beasts.

These animals were everywhere, and they all behaved very naturally, being animals, but were never frightened by his presence. In fact, when they saw him, he was pretty sure they had expected him. He was pretty sure they would have offered themselves to him for dinner if they thought he was suffering from malnutrition. They seemed that nice.

On a side note, one particular thing Darius' new home was absolutely devoid of: Advertising. There were no billboards anywhere. There were no magazines, no newspapers, no internets, or televisions. There were also no buildings, or roads, or cars, or power lines, or planes or engines of any sort making noise. He had traveled far enough with no signs of civilization that he assumed he was alone. Darius was fine without civilization. Other people might not be so bad. For instance, memories of his sister were the only lingering sadness in his heart or mind. Other people, he could love. Civilization could take a hike and stay there.

As he travelled, Darius eventually understood he was moving with a purpose. Whatever he was on his way to see, it called him, or lead him, or let's just say he was headed straight for it one way or another. But his destination was far away, that's for sure. He had a long way to go and had already walked many days. Along the way he got stronger. Darius grew healthier and happier than he'd ever been. And still he walked. On and on. It felt to Darius as if wherever he was when he arrived through the mysterious doorway, he had wound up on the complete opposite side of the planet from wherever he was supposed to be. He was correct. Purpose.

9

Tom didn't know why he'd been chosen. The old brown fellow found him in the gym in 1959, as Tom watched himself miss the free-throws of the National Championship game again. This wasn't by choice. This wasn't some attempt to punish himself. I suppose one might call it fate. After Darius and Daffodil had returned home on the first day they'd all met, Tom returned to the thing-uh-muh-what's-it in the woods and walked right on through, slave to the goddess of compulsion.

Tom missed the free-throws yet again.

"How'd ya like a chance to hit those?"

Tom jumped as if he had seen another ghost. He turned in the direction of the voice, and what he actually saw was an old fella with a dark complexion. The old man smiled.

"You can see me?" asked Tom.

"Sure I can young man. I brought ya here."

"You brought me here?"

"Well, sort of. For yer sake, yes. I'm in charge of the portal ya went through, and others like it. What made ya do that?"

"I don't know," said Tom.

"Figures," said the man. Then he looked up towards the ceiling of the gym and said, "Thanks a lot."

"What did you mean, would I like a chance to hit those?"

"Oh, I don't mean go back in time or nothin like that," said the old man. "Though I s'pose we could. Sorta already are. Half-way there anyway. No, I was speakin more along the lines of doin somethin with yerself. Maybe help ya let go all this a little bit." The old man opened his arms wide to the scene at hand, as Tom missed the foul shots one more time.

"What sort of thing are you talking about mister? Who are you?"

"That's complicated, but I'm a friend Tom. That ya can trust. I'm a friend, and I need yer help. I think yer gonna wanna help me too, when I tell ya what it's all about."

"Well then sir, I suppose that's what you ought to do and we'll see."

"Fair enough young fella, fair enough. Let's take a walk while we talk. Was hard enough watchin ya miss those shots the first time 'round." The old man chuckled softly through a wry smile as he led Tom out of the gym.

We're back with Daffodil, the day her brother Darius went through the portal. Daffodil stopped crying, rose, and re-visited her interest in following Darius into the cloud thing (what we now know to be a portal, and henceforth, referred to as such). She stepped in the portal's direction.

"I don't think you're supposed to do that yet," said Tom. He's standing behind Daffodil.

"He can't go," she said. The sound of her voice made Tom's stomach turn.

"He's gone sweetie, and you won't be able to find him." Tom's new job sucked.

"Why?"

Another stomach turn. "Because they don't work that way."

"How do you know?" She trembled.

Ugh. Heart wrenching. "Because I was in there."

After he convinced her it wasn't the right time to go look for her brother, Tom walked Daffodil home. Along the way, he explained to Daffodil that Darius was safe and that she had to trust him. The girl had questions, of course, but Tom assured her they would have more opportunities to chat.

Tom didn't explain to Daffodil how important she was, or how when she was ready she would indeed go looking for her brother. He didn't try to explain hardly any of what the old stranger had told him. This wasn't the time. The girl was only nine years old, after all, and not yet ready to confront destiny's fuckery head-on. So, Tom convinced her to go on back home. To go on back home and take the beatings from her daddy a while longer, and to let her momma keep abusing her too, both mentally and physically. Basically, Tom sent Daffodil back into hell. To be fair, he felt like shit about it.

10

What's really going on here? I'm trapped in a room. It is a small room with too many walls and not enough windows. As in no windows.

I'm surrounded by clocks. They don't tell me what time it is because they don't know. They only know what time they are, and every damn hand on every damn clock is giving me the middle finger.

These asshole clocks are simply here to remind me of the concept of time in general. As of right now, in this room, my life is not prey to any of the restrictions the concept of time finds necessary. I'm on a mission. I am being forced to write a book. This book. It doesn't matter what the book is about. That's up to me. It doesn't matter if the book is a good read. All that matters is I complete my assignment. Oh, it also has to be true and sincere. Yeah.

I'm lonely. I am trapped in this room with no one to talk to except Bob and whomever will eventually read this. I apologize if the story of my favorite person is sprinkled with a little personal dialogue between you and I, but as I said, I (I, I, I, I...) have no one else to talk to, and I'm afraid I'm going to lose my mind before I can get this finished. If I go crazy, I don't think my work will be approved.

I'm afraid I'm already going crazy. Now you know what's really going on here.

11

This girl's brain scares the shit out of me. That's what Bobby Gout was thinking as he stared down the long, seemingly endless hallway of doors in front of him. If he were to turn around and stare directly behind him, he would see the same damn thing. Robert A. Gout is a hero. He's also my friend, and the younger brother of Mr. Curtis Gout, celestial agent, controller of portals, and the poor fella who's currently trapped in some old lady's jigsaw puzzle.

Interesting fact: The universe has a machine that writes the autobiography of every living soul in its body. That's correct, I said autobiography, because the recordings are written from each person's point of view with their own dialect, vocabulary, personality, and all the little quirks that make you, you. Your thoughts are recorded as a narrative. Thousands of interstellar voice-artists have been recruited over the years to narrate the audiobook versions. Bob's a jogger. Likes to listen on the run…

As you're reading this right now, somewhere out there your soul is making a recording of doing so, telling your story the way you would. Of course there is major editing involved, as none of us live lives where every detail is worthy of record. Still, someday when you die you might have the chance to hear some famous dead person narrate you reading this book, from your perspective, and most likely exclaiming, "What the fuck is going on here?"

Why would the Lord our Bob do this? Mostly just to have things on file. Besides, eternity is a very long time. There are a lot of souls out there with a lot of hours on their hands and not a lot to do. At least this way they will always have something to read. Plus, Bob is omniscient, which means he is well aware of the fact that someday someone is going to want him to prove he's all-knowing. Well, if you've written the autobiography of every soul in the universe, I would say that's pretty solid proof.

How do I know about this machine? I was given access to help with my assignment, but my connection seems to be fritzing in and out. I was able to pick up this feed on Bobby Gout, so I'm going to cheat a little bit and do some intentional plagiarizing. I thought I would let you get to know Bobby on his terms, from his point of view. I've cobbled the upcoming passage together from Bobby's feed. He's never been much of a talker, so he might kill me for doing this. If you knew him personally you would understand what a treat this is. Anyway, without further ado, meet Bobby Gout.

This girl's brain scares the shit out of me. There are hundreds of doorways to other worlds hidden inside the mind of a child. They usually close as the child grows. Sometimes they remain open, leaving a mind to the whims of other creatures. But this girl's? This girl's mind is a whole other story.

Ghosts and spirits – which are not the same thing, despite what some might tell you – often find homes inside a child's head. Demons, alien symbionts, witch doctors, formless energies. All these things may take root inside a child when they're young. Most only looking for a nice place to hide. It's like watching television. Nestle up to the cerebellum and enjoy the show. But there are thieves too. Soul vultures. They're the enemy. They don't just enjoy the ride, they use and abuse. There's one in particular, The One, a bastard child of the cosmos who's growing in strength. I will find him.

The cretin's from another universe, and his evil can only be accurately described in the languages of the worlds he comes from. Those worlds lost their war with him. Now he's their ruler, and he's gone to war with us. In our worlds he calls himself Timmy. Sometimes he's a child, others he's a man, always he's a monster. He fancies himself a "God." He's no god.

The monster imprisoned my brother Curtis – where I do not know – and stole the gateways Curtis was chosen to protect. Timmy trapped their magic in an amulet around his wrist. Now the gateways answer to his insane will. I followed him here, inside this child's head. Now I'm lost.

The real God, the ruler of all that is, the creator of our universe, and Timmy's I presume, I don't know who or what he is and I don't give a shit. I do know this. He can do whatever the hell he wants. Benevolent? Whatever. Do you truly understand the concept of being able to do whatever you want? Do you understand the possibilities? Are you scared to ask the questions? Don't mistake what I consider pragmatism as contempt. Whoever's running this show has to be on our side. That's all we can hope, but I'll be damned if he doesn't make it hard sometimes.

Back to the point, endless possibilities. Take for example our concept of the universe, or even smaller, our galaxy. The Milky Way is bigger than the average person can truly fathom. We've traveled to outer-space, yet barely beyond the reaches of our own gravity. And here I am, standing in an alternate dimension hidden inside the mind of a child. Somewhere in these hallways is the door to the most sacred place in our universe. The most sacred of all universes. That's what Timmy's after, and that's what I must find.

The first time I met Timmy feels like ages ago. Back then I had no idea about nothing but the struggle to survive in our ego-maniacal society, and Timmy had no understanding for what he was. When I met him, his name was Gladys and he was a man. He was a six and a half foot tall Chinaman, bald as a pecker and meaner than my mother.

I was younger then, early twenties. I'd travelled to Los Angeles to find my fame and fortune. Wound up in a restaurant serving rich people to make my bills. Nice place, but it catered to a crowd you might consider a little rougher than others. There was a ton of old money flowing through that restaurant. Most the people tossing the dough around were legit, but anywhere you find high stacks of cash you'll find the criminal element.

When I'm talking about money, I'm telling you this was one of those places where the rich came to play and no one said no. Drugs, gambling, whores. All were available under the guise of a four star restaurant. There was a basement level with private rooms and separate entrances most of the hoods preferred. Not Gladys though. Gladys had to be out in the open. With just enough legitimate business dealings, nobody really questioned where he made his money, even if they all knew deep down he was dirty. One of those rare criminals that the upper crust accepted. Either from fear, or morbid curiosity, or simply to live vicariously through someone who was willing to wield power that didn't come from a bank account. Power that comes from personal will, which was the only sort of power men like Gladys truly cared about. A lot of people throw money around. It's a rare few who dominate the world around them through shear force of will.

As I said, I was serving tables there, waiting for something better to come along. One night, after a long day of kissing way too many asses, the wrong thing happened at just the right time. It was fairly common for some of the clowns that came there with pockets full of cash to have too much drink, or too many trips to the bathroom to shove junk up their nose, and eventually lose their cool, but not in the main dining room. Bullshit was off limits in the main dining room. That was the rule. The dining room made the place legit, and the rule was expected to be respected.

I can admit to not always being the most patient fellow, and someday my temper may very well be my downfall, but this joker had pain coming to him. Women were available for cash, no secret to those who needed to know. But the waitresses were strictly hands off. No exceptions. So this louse starts mouthing off. Some guy I'd seen before, and I knew he was loosely connected, but he was one of those guys on the fringe. His name was Nico Terelli. Nico was a lapdog to anyone that mattered and a bully to anyone that didn't, and the type of person I despise the most. Well he starts in with this pretty little waitress, Sally Kirkmont. She was a sweet girl. Timid as can be. This jackass is trying to drag her off downstairs in front of families with their children, and other people who had no business knowing what really went on inside this place. Sally doesn't know what to do so she starts crying and saying no. Looking around for anyone to help her. Of course no one does.

I probably shouldn't have broken Nico's nose. I could have easily taken him down without hitting him, but I wanted to. He deserved worse.

That's when Gladys noticed me. The giant china-man walked by while Nico was on the floor bleeding, smiled, and handed me a piece of paper with a phone number on it. Maybe I shouldn't have broken Nico's nose. I definitely shouldn't have dialed that number.

I went to work for Gladys the next day, after I was fired from the restaurant for punching Nico. Sally was fired too. I felt a little bad for her but she was safer that way. Hopefully she headed back to whatever safe part of middle-America she'd come from. Nico would have taken his revenge on her eventually. He was that sort of spiteful prick.

Gladys made me a courier to start, but I moved up through his ranks fairly quick. I wound up one of his top enforcers. I don't know how I justified that life. I suppose it gave me the opportunity to take my anger out on people who most likely deserved what they got.

The more I learned about Gladys the more I hated him. This was one of those no-win situations in life. Funny how we wind up there. You go about your business, try to do things right, see a chance to try and help somebody weaker than you and the next thing you know you've become the worst part of humanity, and it really feels like it all happened just like that. Like it happened *to* you. Odd really. I'm not saying I don't take responsibility, but sometimes life is a trailer park in a tornado. You chose to live there. You know tornadoes love saying hi, but you hoped for the best. Do you blame yourself while your being swept away in the storm? Maybe so, maybe not.

The stories I could tell about my time with Gladys are not the sort I choose to share. They're part of my life that is filled with shame. I need those memories, but they're mine. Not for everyone. Maybe someday I'll feel like I've earned the right to tell those stories with the humility of someone who knows they've done all they can to right the wrongs of their past. What is most important however, is how I came to truly understand Gladys. How I released his evil on our world, our universe.

Another woman had the misfortune of instigating the end to my Earthly dealings with Gladys, bringing things full circle, I suppose. Unfortunately, this woman I loved. Her name was Cilia, and she belonged to Gladys. I could tell that story, the story of our love and its irresistible force, but you've seen it and heard it a thousand times if once ever. There was no forethought or scheming involved. We saw each other and there was no holding back. Just like a Hollywood romance, blah, blah, blah. It's the gist of this story that matters, and the gist is Gladys killed Cilia, I killed Gladys, and Timmy's newly awakened, black-hearted anti-soul was released into the universe of light. I do apologize.

Sorry, but that's all the Bobby you get. Anymore dipping into his head and he will definitely beat the piss out of me, if I ever see him again. Besides, suddenly I'm not certain I can trust the machine. I just read some of my own thoughts, out of curiosity, and they were not my thoughts at all, unless I'm lying to myself. Either way, I'm hungry. Time for lunch.

12

This story is not about religion, I promise. That said, in this room filled with punitive clocks, I have a lot of time on my hands. When I'm not writing I've been reading, which we all know, as expressed thousands of times in science fiction novels alone, is dangerous business.

The funny thing about the Bible are its contradictions, which begin in Genesis.

Wait, hold that thought. Obviously not everyone believes in the Bible. Sorry. Let's make sure to attend to everyone here, including in brief, religions on other worlds.

If you think shit is bad on Earth, it is. For some reason, religious populations throughout the rest of the universe, according to my records, are way more cool. Not perfect, oh no. But comparatively, way more cool. Thus, we're going to focus here, for a moment, on the stupidity of mankind. The "in brief" portion of our show is now complete. Onto those other, non-Abraham loving, Earth based religions.

What about Hinduism? To my knowledge, I don't really know any Hindus. I have one confirmed meeting with a Hindu male, a coworker at the time, whose presence I thoroughly enjoyed, but, and unrelated to my enjoyment of his company, he didn't follow any of the Hindu rules. I assume I come in contact with other Hindu practitioners fairly regularly when back on Earth. There are tons of Hindus, but they also have a lot of gods. I'm over simplifying here, as some Hindu philosophy harkens everything back to a form of monotheism, but it's all so complicated, and somehow there is room for atheism in the Hindu faith as well. When atheism got involved, that's where I stopped reading. For brevity's sake, and the sake of my sardonic argument, let's just agree there are shitloads of Hindus and shitloads of Hindu gods, so when you make it a ratio of believer to deity, the Hindus don't really stack up, percentage-wise, to all those who believe in the Bob associated with the Abrahamic religions.

While we're dealing with the "non-Abrahams" here for a moment, we must include Buddhism as well, though I think Buddhism was intended to be a philosophy, not a religion. But that's not Buddha's fault I suppose. Seems like he was a pretty cool guy, so we'll give Buddhism a pass, which is a major step forward for me 'cause I used to think Buddha was a jerk.

Lastly, before someone makes note of my omission of Sikhism, here they are. Say hello to the Sikhs, at one time, and possibly still, the fifth largest religion on Earth, just behind Buddhism. Sikh philosophy seems fairly peaceful and sensible, perhaps only surpassed in those two areas by the Bahá'í, but then again, all these religions are made of humans…

Even Buddhists and Sikhs have sects with histories of violence, which makes perfect sense, of course. Bobdamn humans.

Along with these massive non-Abrahamic religions are countless other groups with belief systems. There are millions upon millions of people and creatures throughout the universe who have no interest in the rules and regulations of someone else's version of Bob. To be clear, among the Big Three, our beliefs don't matter. We don't count.

Now, back to the Big Three monotheists on my planet: Christianity, Islam, and Judaism. Christianity and Islam are the largest worldwide. Judaism is actually the sixth largest religion on Earth at the time of this writing, but when I say "the Big Three," I'm not just talking membership numbers. I'm talking historical context and ego. The Hindus, Buddhists, and Sikhs just don't make enough noise!

Anyway, the Big Three all dig the Old Testament, and they all have their own version of Adam and Eve, the original sinners. The very first to tell Bob to go fuck himself when confronted with a successful marketing pitch. Oh that slippery serpent salesman.

So, whether or not you cop to the dogma of original sin or not, all three Abrahamic religions basically agree mankind was given free will to fuck up as much as we want and reap the wonderfully horrible consequences (Often wonderful up front on Earth, with some pretty shitty horrible to be reaped on the back end). Here's the rub. If Bob were infallible and all powerful, didn't she know free will would makes humans deny her? Did she not foresee our ruin? Why bother with the whole production in the Garden of Eden? She made us the way we are, broken, then set us up for failure? She made us the way we are, yet *we* were incapable of just enjoying the Eden we'd been given without breaking the rules? Free will, you say? She made us the way we are! Jerk.

By the way, don't get me started on how sexist that whole deal is, at least for the Christians. For the ladies, I won't ignore the unfairness and lack of political correctness involved in blaming all of man's problems on the mischievous female, or the fact that the original mother actually came from man. Just a tasty rib.

Yes, it was a testosterone driven universe in those times.

My point is Bob's plan seems more convoluted than a bad movie's villainous plot. It is ridiculously confusing. How could Bob have the power to create the entirety of existence yet perform as such an ineffective leader? Or is she just winging it? Is it possible we have a trial and error administration running things around here? There's no plan? Eep!

Now, according to the Big Three, Bob has a plan, and at some point that plan insists upon the idea that only one religion can be the correct answer. (To be fair, I only know the Koran and numerous Judaic texts on a cursory level, quite intentionally. I'm basing my argument on practical observation). Of course the various leaders will all say their religion is the one true faith, though each faith is peppered with a few rascals who are willing to admit Bob might cut folks who practiced the incorrect faith with extreme fervor some slack. Me personally, I must admit if any religion ever came out and said, "You know what, I think those other guy's actually got it right, but we're gonna keep doing our thing," I'm fairly certain I would join the religion that was admitting they got it wrong. Humility goes a long way with sarcastic assholes.

So, if all the most contentious religions insist they're the only one that is correct, this makes everyone else wrong. Even if they are gracious to each other, it's that Earthman, Southern United States grace that often oozes contempt through the smiliest of white teeth. They all insist that Bob would go to the trouble of making all these other people, these other believers, simply to cast them aside. Or, if not cast aside, they get to ride the proverbial bench in purgatory until they decide to play for the correct team. "Jones, if you've accepted our version of the truth then get in the game. You've been blessed."

Basically, the Big Three all insist that Bob is a crazy male asshole with a wicked vindictive streak. An elitist of the highest caliber who struts through the universe with his nose pointed upwards while his chosen few clamor behind him kissing his heals, his ass, and anything else they can pucker-up to while attempting to ensure their spot in eternity, all the while blustering about faith as they sin their Bob-damned asses off.

Real faith is denying all you've been taught. Real faith is breaking rules that are clearly bullshit. Real faith is not knowing, it's hoping.

I really shouldn't be talking about this. I have the universe to save. Besides, what do I know about faith?

Real faith is a continuous search for the proof you need to believe, even though you know you will never find it, just because you so truly, honestly, sincerely (I mean you really mean it) want to believe.

That is real faith. You may disagree with me, but trust me. I know. I had my faith shattered. When something gets shattered, you know that shit was real.

Why was my faith shattered? Because my faith was in not knowing. I wasn't a believer, and unfortunately, I found proof. Faith is, in and of itself, a concept highly reliant on lack of proof.

Please don't quit on me. Not yet. I promise, this story is not about religion.

13

Daffodil was sixteen years old, her diary filled with passages about losing her mind. Sadly, she was. Seven years had passed since Darius ran away. She barely spoke anymore. Speaking felt like a waste of time.

She was thin, with long, deep brown hair. Her eyes wide-open blue. She was beautiful, but she didn't know, and certainly didn't feel that way. You could see the woman she would become hidden behind her burdens. This was the girl I would meet. This was the girl I would fall blindly for. I remember seeing all that pain, finding her so lovely yet so sad, and feeling desperate to make her pain go away. The moment I saw her my heart started flipping in my chest and has never stopped.

After her brother ran away, her parents' irrational and uncontrolled emotional outbursts grew more vindictive. Over time, the loss of Darius became Daffodil's fault. Forget the way they had treated the boy. In hindsight he was their greatest treasure, and their abuse of Daffodil was laced with a new level of contempt.

If growing into womanhood with no guidance wasn't hard enough to deal with, if being abused by her parents wasn't hard enough to deal with, imagine going through puberty while a thousand voices echoed in your head. Imagine making that weirdly frustrating transition into physical adulthood while your sub-conscious was continuously being sliced and diced into a stream of multiple personalities. Some were good, others bad, all of them struggled for control. Now imagine an army of you in your mind, fighting a house full of invaders. Imagine all these other pieces of you, good or bad, united in a battle against foreign invaders, and the prize is your mind, if it survives the battle. This is what life was like for the woman I love.

When she slept, she had visions of her brother. Darius started visiting her about a year after he disappeared. The visions quickly came and went. Daffodil couldn't tell where he was but he seemed happy. In her dreams it felt like Darius was trying to talk to her, to comfort her, but she couldn't hear him through all the shouting and fighting in her mind.

When she was awake, Daffodil spent most of her time in motion. Movement and activity kept her in charge. Staying busy was the only way to quiet the storm. Meanwhile, the beatings continued.

Daffodil was pulled out of public school after the first time a teacher noticed her bruises. Her parents wouldn't let her have friends. The only way to keep a secret is to keep it, and they needed their punching bag. Daffodil remained at home, a slave to their every whim.

Tom watched Daffodil grow. There were times he intervened to save her life from her parent's abuse. But if not a life or death situation, he was disallowed contact. Communication wasn't safe. If he communicated with her, the temporal rift created might attract the wrong attention.

I will admit to you, I believe Tom loved her every bit as much as I do. That's a hard thing for a man to admit about the woman he loves, but I know it's true. Tom stayed with her and cared for her, and all the while she never knew. He was her only friend. If Tom the ghost had been able to cry during those years, he might never have stopped.

Daffodil never closed her eyes. No matter what her parents did to her, she never stopped watching. This was her only revenge. She knew they were monsters, but even monsters have memories. Until the end of their days and on into eternity, those horrible, worthless pieces of breathing garbage would forever see Daffodil's emotionless face, watching what they did to her.

I don't want to discuss this anymore.

14

Listen up 'cause this part is quick. I've uncovered some old transference records. I'm going to explain how Timmy wound up inside a Chinaman named Gladys.

Timmy escaped his universe by throwing himself into a quasar and riding the light. The ray of light he caught was a celestial bridge that souls travel from one destination to the next. Call it the Celestial Soulway, and think of it as a soul super highway through the cosmos. There's a soul-pool lane and everything.

Timmy wound up piggybacking an unfortunately gentle soul mistakenly assigned to Earth. Earth was home to the nastiest collection of souls in the universe, except for Hates, though Hates is mostly full of Earthlings, so, you know…

Seriously, if you wind up on Earth you're either on a mission from Bob, you're being punished for doing something bad, or like the soul Timmy hijacked, you were accidentally fucked by the universe.

Get outside the Milky Way and ask around sometime. Here's a telling point: Most of the people I know on Earth would agree that the world is full of jerks.

So anyway, that's how Timmy arrived. A fly by soul jacking. The soul Timmy hitched a ride on was bound for China, where it wound up inside a fetus that would eventually become an abnormally large Chinese fellow named Gladys. In hindsight, when an energy spike occurred during the soul's final transmission before life-cycle inception, the abnormality should have been reported by the recording technician, but even celestial bureaucracy has folks asleep at the wheel.

As it turns out, the human body was an excellent incubator for Timmy's evil, though somewhat of a prison as well. Timmy wasn't in control, instead playing the role of evil, spiritually cancerous spectator. He was trapped inside that Earthly body, which he completely corrupted, until my friend Bobby Gout killed Gladys and unleashed Timmy on our universe. That wasn't Bobby's fault though. As I said before he's a hero, at least in my book. Bobby did not know it at the time, but he was only doing his job. Bob's will and what not.

When Timmy first escaped Earth and began hunting the destruction of our existence he was still a child. Indeed, his hatred for our universe was pure childish contempt from the beginning. With no one to spank him, his contempt never felt the warm hand of correction. Timmy was never dealt an attitude adjustment. So, he would remain an insolent child throughout his existence.

Although he knew what he wanted, Timmy had absolutely no idea how to carry out the destruction of our universe. In fact, when he first arrived, Timmy had very little thought at all. For many ages he was a creature driven purely by his unrelenting emotions. The one thing he knew for certain, the one thing he thought over and over, was that he wanted to destroy everything around him.

Time and again we've proven evil exists. The Devil has his minions and they like to stir the drink. Yet Satan has no place in this story other than to say that for once, something shitty was going on and that prick was not really involved, though he has taken credit for Timmy's handiwork on numerous occasions.

The Devil is a dick. I've met him. He has nowhere near the power over us he would like us to believe. He has nowhere near the power of Timmy. Satan likes to profess he could have manipulated Timmy and wielded his power if he had chose, but for this adventure the Devil was nothing more than a homeowner in a trailer park, just waiting and hoping.

Despite whatever enjoyment old Beelzebub might have typically felt in a situation such as this, he knew that if Timmy got what he wanted it would be the end of Hell as well. That was the power of Timmy. This isn't foreshadowing by the way, just a chance to remind the Devil of his limitations. He'll be reading, trust me.

Evil must be nurtured, and Timmy was meant to be evil. Evil was his corner of the room. Eventually, a very large corner in a very large room. Once he was free to travel our universe, he wandered from planet to planet consuming souls and gaining knowledge.

Timmy learned all manner of things unwholesome and reviled from the souls he consumed, as he preferred dark matter.

That's a physicist joke. I have no idea if it is functional, if it equates. I was gonna say "he preferred dark meat," inspired by thoughts of a preference when one eats chicken or turkey, but I was afraid I might be taken the wrong way.

Despite Timmy's sinister nature and the ages of knowledge he acquired, we were dealt one saving grace, perhaps the only thing that left us any hope whatsoever. He remained completely inept in times of decisiveness. Timmy, if his existence were more commonly known throughout the universe, would have gone down as the absolute worst clutch performer throughout the history of history.

15

Darius' body was now sixteen years old. For seven years he'd walked in infinite bliss, often moving as slowly as possible. During that time, he discovered he could speak with the animals. Not with his voice. Darius hadn't spoken a word aloud since his arrival. They thought to one another, sharing their emotions, their states of being. These animals were no different than Darius. They were souls trapped inside bodies that walked and breathed. Gentle souls that had survived the trappings of self-awareness unscathed, and were rewarded for their innocence with the most peaceful existence possible. Praise Bob, I suppose.

The only aspect of his former life Darius hadn't completely forgotten was Daffodil. As he traveled, Darius realized he could feel her. The connection was different for Darius than the visions Daffodil had of him. While she saw him in her sleep, Darius communicated with her when he was awake. He thought to her as one might a deceased loved one, and when he did he worried over her like a flustered parent.

From what I can tell, he didn't know why or how he knew Daffodil, or why he was so constantly worried for her, but he didn't waste time with questions. All that was important was she was there, a picture in his mind. An image attached to an emotion. Love. His heart told him to love her, to soothe her, and to tell her everything was going to be okay. To his constant dismay, he had no idea if she could hear him.

During his journey, the balance between his mind and body reached a peak that was simply impossible for any other creature in any other place than this. The very cells he was made of could "speak" to him. If Darius had ever gone back to his home, people would still have perceived him as autistic. Despite his physical conditioning, and his elaborate mind, he would have remained silent. If he spoke he would've been taken for a retard – a very unfortunate term, especially when Darius was simply operating from a level of consciousness that humans were ill-prepared to understand. Of course, this is all conjecture, as Darius did not return to Earth. My purpose in mentioning this is two fold. First, never discount the significance of things you don't understand, like people with supposed disabilities, when it comes to the existential workings of the Bob. And second…

Here, in this place, Darius was what he was intended to be. He trained his body to move in a thousand different ways on instinct. He developed the perfect union between his muscles, his mind, his energy, and his soul. No thought was required for this transformation. No planning was involved. The change happened so naturally, he scarcely noticed until the metamorphosis was complete, though every once in awhile he stopped whatever he was doing and realized his face hurt from smiling so hard. Darius, despite his ever-present smile and pleasant disposition, was becoming a weapon.

Darius laid on his back and stared at the most magnificent thing he'd ever seen. True, his frame of reference might have been lacking. His short life wasn't filled with memories of wonderful moments and beautiful sights, but he was certain there was nothing more fantastic anywhere in existence. He'd found his destination. Upon arrival, he had no idea what to do other than lie there and stare, and enjoy, so that's what he did.

16

Have I told you yet about how I met Bob? I suppose not, though I did foreshadow the hell out of this chapter at the end of my previous rant about religion and faith. Sort of let the cat out of the bag for the sequel too, but that story is at least two books away, and while I doubt either of my next two masterpieces will save the universe, I must exercise the demons I was blessed with.

At the time of this writing I haven't met Bob yet, per say. I just know that I will because a future me told me so. I didn't care much for future me. Very smug.

Anyway, future me said that whatever the hell Bob is, when I meet Bob, he, she, or it will tell me I can call him or her or it whatever I want. Cool guy girl thing, Bob.

Can we just agree to call him her for the time being, for simplicity's sake, and duly note that the concept of a creator is truly gender unspecific, thus allowing us to move along with my damn story happily knowing I'm only mildly chauvinistic and think any opposite sex has just as much right to claim our creator for their gender? Sheesh.

Yes, I met the me that met her, and had a long talk with the future me. Here are the highlights:

"You know I'm not supposed to be telling you this," I said. "It's breaking the rules."

"Then why are you?" I asked.

"Because she told me to," I said.

It's just that sort of nonsense that insists I omit the rest of the conversation between myself and I, at least for the time being. I found myself chock-full of pretention, and am now extremely cautious of avoiding development in that department for the rest of my natural life.

Do you know what I actually said to myself? "We're all here to teach each other. Who's here to learn?" Can you believe that tripe? I mean, who does my future self think he is, or who I may someday be? The nerve.

Now, I'm going to tell you this because I think you should know, but I don't want you to be unsettled. As a matter of fact, I think if you look at the upcoming revelation the correct way, you should find comfort in what I'm about to tell you. Here's what I am going to tell you – I hope you are sitting down and if not, at least not holding anything sharp. No, you should definitely be sitting down AND not holding anything sharp because here is what I am going to tell you:

Even Bob doesn't know what "It" is all about. Take a deep breath. Remain calm.

Bob doesn't know where she is from, she doesn't know who made her, and she painfully, unmistakably, unequivocally does not know what "It" is all about. So if you think she is just being mean, that she's been holding out on us all this time trying to make us earn the right to know, well folks, just let it go. She's "all knowing" and still can't figure it out.

"But wait," you say. "How can God be all knowing and not know what 'It' is all about?"

First, this is why Bob, in her infinite wisdom, told me I could call her whatever I want. God's name should be something more comfortable, like Bob, when dealing with her fallacies. Bob is a very cozy name.

So how can Bob be all knowing and not know what "It" is all about?

See, isn't that more comfortable? It's a lot easier to deal with a deity named Bob who doesn't know what "It" is all about.

How can Bob not know where she's from? How can Bob not know who made her? The answer: The Unknowable.

Still confused? No? Either way, let me explain.

As we've already learned from my prophetic unnamed friend through the retelling of Timmy's origin, this and every other universe sustain themselves through maintaining a delicate balance of existence. For every thing, there is no thing. For every same, there is a not so much alike. So, for all there is to know, there is an equal amount of the unknowable.

If you are now lamenting Bob's omniscience, lament no longer. She is definitely all-knowing. Bob knows everything that is knowable among all the known universes.

Of course, if you are paying attention, you might ask, "Known universes? Would that imply there are unknown universes? Or at least imply that is a valid question?" Ah-ha! Now we're cooking with butter. Yes, many scholars now assume the existence of universes unknown to Bob, which raises the question of things to be known within those unknown universes, a field of study that might eventually prove Bob un-all-knowing, though The Unknown Universes Theory of Limitations On Bob is currently a strictly conceptual school of thought being researched at the University For The Study Of The Reality Of The Unknown.

What we do know, or at least have delicately surmised, is that if Bob did know the unknowable, the balance of the known and unknown would be broken, and existence would implode. Bob might survive, though I personally find that doubtful. Humanity would definitely be cockroach food, as everyone knows cockroaches can survive anything. When everything falls apart, the cockroaches will be partying in Las Vegas.

So, the next time you are feeling cheated because you don't get to know everything, take this into consideration. As a human, we only have to "not know" for a hundred years or so if we're lucky. Bob has to "not know" for eternity, and she has to live with the reality that if she ever found out, she might destroy existence. She has to spend eternity actively avoiding learning too much. That might not be too hard for us. I think it's probably a challenge for the creator of everything.

So, the next time you feel air for the words "Why God Why?" gather in your lungs, do us all a favor and bite your fucking tongue.

Remind yourself that if Bob knew why, existence would most likely crumble, then please let go of your petty emotions, or someday, Bob might grow weary of existence and decide to find the answer to your question.

17

There is one perfect place.

One.

When Bob realized that sentient beings weren't capable of incorruptible wholesomeness, she knew there should be at least one place that exemplified purity. She needed one pure creation in her body of work. Something to help counteract all the evil in the universe. You see, many of her firstborn, most wholesome souls were getting old and tired. They grew weary from their constant battle with evil and needed a place to rest. Then Bob realized she was getting old, and a little tired, and that eventually she would need a place to rest. She had tried so hard with all of her people, including humans, but we always came out broken. Every time she fixed one thing, something else would go wrong, until she finally understood why she couldn't make us perfect, and why we couldn't be happy all the time: Self-awareness.

Consider how sad this must have made her. Can't quite picture it? Try harder. Think about death. Better yet, imagine giving birth to a child and raising it everyday of its life with unconditional love. Then imagine how confusing and painful and fucked up life would be if your child turned out to be a cannibalistic serial killer. I imagine everyday must be like that for Bob.

Bob needed something pure in her. Something perfect, gentle, beautiful and strong. Something to make her feel better when the rest of her felt bad. Plus, she needed something to ensure that her body would carry on if her mind ever faltered. A universal pace-maker. This is what she made: A planet of perfection. Bob's most beautiful piece of work to date. There are mountains, oceans, valleys, rivers, islands and every animal from every planet of her entire universe. Also every plant and insect from every planet. Bob took everything she'd ever created except people and put all that stuff in one magnificent place. A place so magnificent, so unknown by anyone save for Bob and a few lucky retired souls, that this place doesn't even have a name.

For the purposes of this story, this wonderful place needs a name. I can't exactly call it the place with "mountains and oceans and valleys and rivers and islands and every animal from every planet of her entire universe and every plant and insect from every planet of her entire universe" all the way through this book. The problem is, there are no words in my language let alone any other language I am privy to that would justly describe the beauty, wonder, and unfathomable innocence that is this planet. For my own amusement and the logistical purposes of relaying this story to you, during a week of unfathomable boredom, I set myself to creating such a word.

The result? I've named the planet Euphoratopadopia, and on Euphoratopadopia is one object that embodies all that is wholesome and righteous. This object is the most beautiful, most splendid, most perfect part of the most perfect place in the universe. You may have heard of it before in legend or folklore. Some call it the Tree of Life. Others call it the Tree of Souls. It is definitely a tree. I call it Kyle.

18

This is the same thing twice, but different. Yes, Euphoratopadopia is that important. Kyle is that important.

There is one perfect place in the universe. Only one. Its perfection is not a metaphor, not simply in the eye of a beholder or the innocence of a child's heart. This is genuine, I'll-be-damned-If-I-didn't-think-it-was-impossible, perfection. Euphoratopadopia is the only place where life exists that has not grown ugly. The only place in existence unsoiled by the narcissistic nature of self-awareness. Indeed, the word "I" has never been uttered in this most wonderful place.

When things started to go wrong in our universe, when Bob realized the reality of her situation, she was overcome with sadness. Everything she created had flaws. Existence was a work of art in progress she could never walk away from, never declare satisfaction with, never finish.

Imagine her disappointment when her presumed first love, mankind, turned out to be a complete bunch of morons who couldn't even behave themselves in Utopia. – I'm not talking about the Garden of Eden. I'm talking about the Earth in general. Earth was a Utopia, and pretty fucking fantastic until we got our hands on it. Although, to be fair, life didn't go so well anywhere else in the universe either. Apparently, all sentient life forms absolutely refuse to relinquish their Bob given right to behave like jerks. The problem was, the universe needed someplace perfect. Someplace to provide us with enough good energy that we didn't all tumble straight into misery and dysfunction. The universe needed a lifejacket. And on the one million and seventh day, Bob created perfection. Then she took a nap.

Euphoratopadopia's location is a secret, of course. No one, and I mean absolutely no one knows where the planet is located. It's existence is only whispered of in legends. Legends which have taken on their own identities and rely very little on truth. Legends that require maps to be found hidden in attics, if anyone is to ever prove the legends are real.

There is no map. Even Curtis Gout's time, space, and dimension hopping portals can't take you to Euphoratopadopia. And while I'm certain Bob has a few tricks up her sleeves (she always does), the only two paths I'm aware of for travelling to the planet are through soul reassignment or a particular door hidden inside a particular alternate dimension hidden inside a particular...

If anyone knew where the only perfect place in the universe was located, don't you think one of us would trash the place? I would argue that's almost a certainty. Someone would decide they had to conquer it, and/or uncover its secrets for eternal life, and/or use its natural resources to power their engines and/or back their monetary systems.

Bob knows there are infinite justifications for how and why we would screw perfection up, just like we have all our own planets. So, this planet was kept a secret and remained nameless. Until now. I'm assuming if Bob didn't want me talking about this, she wouldn't have let me in on the secret.

As I said earlier, on Euphoratopadopia is Kyle, the Tree of Souls. Kyle is the source of purity for our existence. The embodiment of all the purest souls to have ever existed, removed from their cyclical lives and made a part of the eternal engine that keeps this whole locomotive called existence chugging down the tracks. This tree provides innocence, love, hope, and joy to us all. It breathes these things into creation, giving Bob hope, giving our universe the ability to survive the hardship all of Bob's other creations lay at her cosmic feet.

If a tree on Earth provides oxygen for human beings to live, Kyle provides our universe the "air", the strength, it needs to survive. Without Kyle, the universe would fall into darkness. Without Kyle, Bob could not take the pain. Timmy wants to chop Kyle down.

19

I told you Daffodil never closed her eyes when her parents abused her. They're open now. I'm watching and recording in real time. You'll read this next passage while somewhere the events are currently happening.

Her father's hand smacks her face again and again. Her mother is kicking her and calling her names. Prancing around the room with bottle in hand. The bottle empties and bounces of Daffodil's head onto the floor. Her father's hand strikes again. This time she hears bones in her face crackle. She's thankful for the pain in her face. It distracts from the beating she's taking below the waste.

Daffodil squirms on the kitchen floor, receiving her violence. Booze and drugs. A burnt supper. A punishment countless others have received for countless other reasons, but this girl is mine. I tell you I'm crying right now. All you have to do is read. I have to watch. She has to live this horror.

This is the breaking point, the last beating she can take for a while, maybe ever if they don't stop soon. Daffodil breaks her own rule and closes her eyes. She wonders if this is death. Is she going to die? She's never felt that before. She's always known she was going to make it through. Her anger always held, but not in this moment. In this moment she feels weak, as if she's slipping away.

"Run."

She hears but doesn't believe her ears.

"Daffodil, run."

It's a kind voice she thinks she knows, but she feels dead. She feels numb. The voice has to be her imagination.

"Daffodil, please wake up."

She's not asleep but her eyes won't open. Daffodil's not here or there or anywhere. She's somewhere in between all those places, falling. Endlessly falling. Arms flail, reaching, grasping at nothing. Confusion screams at her in a thousand voices, a thousand languages. It's dark white noise. Darkness taking her from her self, stealing her.

"DAFFODIL!"

The scream is heard. A hand wraps around her wrist and slows her fall, but the fall isn't real because she's not awake, not alive anymore. You're too late, whoever you are. Daffodil has landed in her grave.

Then her eyes open. She's alive! Something is pulling on her arm, actually physically pulling, urging her upwards. Up from the grave in her mind. Up from the floor in the kitchen. It's Tom! But he's not real?

"Get up, please," Tom begs. "We've got to go." Things were in place. This was the time.

Daffodil stands. Tom helps her. Mom is slouched over the table. Dad looks mad. He's in the corner rubbing his head and trying to stand. He looks at Daffodil and growls. He's the devil. What did you do Tom?

"DAFFODIL, RUN DAMN IT!"

She's out the door, watching her feet move, accelerating from a shuffle to a clumsy jog. Her lungs swell and cave. Her father is behind her screaming. Her right arm drags the rest of her body. She squints for focus and sees Tom pulling her.

Into the woods they run. Her eyes are closed again as her savior guides her. Branches whip against her face. Leaves crumble under her feet. Father is still coming, still screaming, but his words sound far away, as if he's screaming into a canyon and his words have to bounce their way from wall to wall to her ears. But there's no canyon, and he is much closer than that. Daffodil is not fully present. She's alive in two different worlds, running for her life in both. Tom is pulling her through the woods in the real world. The world you live in, the one I used to.

Tom is calling to her. "It's gonna be hard Daffodil," he screams. "Real hard, but I promise I'm gonna be with you the whole time! I swear! Don't ever despair Daffodil! Not ever! I will always be there!"

She knows Tom is yelling to her but she can't decipher his words. Only her body is running through those woods with Tom. Her mind is splitting time in that other realm, a part of existence that few of us touch but all of us take part in, where Daffodil is running for her life on her own.

This other world is a maze. She looks over her shoulder as she runs. Insanity clamors behind her. Without knowing where she's going, self-preservation insists that she is running to a safe place. There's a safe place ahead and she's going to get there.

Everything is a haze. The hallways. The faces she runs past. The arms – and other things – that reach for her, they're all a blur. They're chasing her. She doesn't know who they are but most of them look like her. Some of them look like monsters and beasts, but most look just like her. There are doors everywhere but none of them will open. These creatures, these ugly versions of her, they grab her and claw at her face. They tear at her clothes but she breaks free. Tom pulls her free as he keeps her body moving forward in the physical world.

My hands are trembling. I don't want to do this anymore.

Tom leads her stumbling through the woods, her father stumbling after. Daffodil is crying and screaming. She's running with Tom but still sees herself fleeing the monsters in her mind. They all hate her so much. They're catching up to her and somehow her father is too. She's tired and can't catch her breath. They're all going to get her.

"Jump!"

In the real world her body leaps into the floating cloud thing. At the same time in that other place, the other world where different versions of her are trying to kill her, a door opens at the end of a hallway. She dives through the door. For an instant she's in both places at once, leaping through both the portal on Earth and the doorway in her mind, crying and bleeding, then darkness.

20

This is the end of Section 1 of this book. Let's review. Daffodil Fields, my wife, was beaten and raped throughout her childhood. There is something wrong with her brain. She is currently the key to our very existence – not the actual key, a ferret has that, she's a metaphorical key – and I'm not just saying that because I love her. She is, in fact, the 1,375,242nd metaphorical key to existence since the Bob started keeping that statistic. Despite being the key to existence, Daffodil is going to die.

Daffodil met a ghost named Tom in the woods outside her home. Tom's a former athlete the universe decided to make a hero. He's Daffodil's guardian. I'm sorry, but Tom is going to die. Again.

Darius is Daffodil's foster brother. He ran away from home and wound up someplace fantastic. Most kids that runaway are not so lucky but Darius is special, although, with apologies, Darius has to die.

Curtis Gout was an old man who's soul got trapped in an old woman's crossword puzzle. He used to control the portals that Tom and Darius and Daffodil went through. I've been through them too by the way, but that is another story for another day. Curtis is my friend. He works for Bob. Curtis is dead-meat.

So's that old lady. She's a goner. And The King is already in a coma, so I think you can guess what his deal is. Just kidding, I don't get to kill The King.

Bobby Gout is Curtis' brother. He's a hero because Bob wants him to atone for his sins. Remember, it's Bob the Omnipotent and Robert "Bobby" Gout the warrior. I know, I know, they're both named Bob and in the same story. Well, one might be God and the other definitely isn't. There, that should do it. It's really not that hard to keep up with. Besides, if you knew how many damned Bobs I've had to keep straight in my head in my life…

Bobby Gout is a murderer. He killed a giant Chinese human whose body was incubating an evil cosmic being named Timmy. Now Bobby's chasing Timmy through an alternate dimension in Daffodil's brain. Bobby Gout is going to die, but he doesn't mind.

Timmy is a cosmic being filled with hatred for our universe. He's chasing a ferret through an alternate dimension in Daffodil's brain. We'll dig further into that situation soon. The gist is Timmy is chasing the ferret because, in the end, Timmy wants to chop down Kyle, the tree of souls, which breathes life into our universe. Timmy is super evil but he's also a complete fuck-up. Thank Bob.

I'm not sure what happens to the ferret but I am 100% certain Section 2 will begin after a short commercial break.

Oh, also, I want to go home. I think maybe I'm losing my mind, but how the fuck am I supposed to confirm my suspicion? Either way, I will not be writing my own death. There, I think that's everyone.

And now, your commercial break.

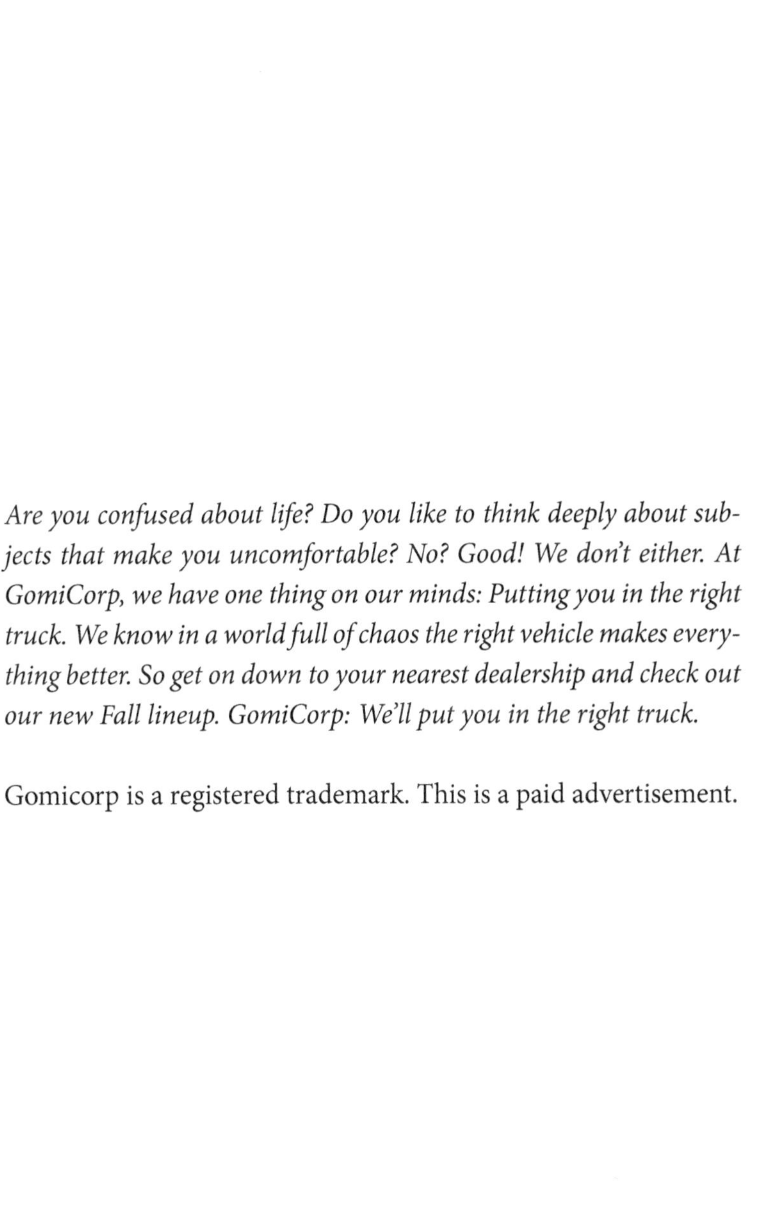

Section 2

21

Please take your seats and feel free to skip this chapter. The story will continue shortly.

It's taken what I think has been a few days for my relative good humor to return. Shortly after I completed Section 1, I threw a bit of a tantrum at Bob. There were tears and fist pounding, foot stomping and screaming, wild accusations of mismanagement, cot kicking, desk flipping, and the hurling of my only chair. But no clock smashing. That was a line my isolated mind somehow knew not to cross, even in my frantically downtrodden state.

This solitude changes a person. Bob is a wonderful listener, but not so much of a talker these days. I don't remember the last time I heard another voice. Meanwhile, Daffodil is still in danger and all I can do is write shit down. Somewhere she is my young lover, asleep in our bed. She's waiting for me to come back or may not even know that I'm gone. Somewhere she is my wife, at home with our children and highly annoyed with the line of work I chose. Somewhere else she is an old widow, marching towards death and our reunion in the afterlife (which, I've unfortunately learned, is no guarantee). But for right now, for this very moment, Daffodil is still a teenage girl, and she's lost. I know she will be safe, but everything I've seen and everything I think I know is subject to change.

The future and the past are written at the same time. The singular aspect of life we know for certain is real is this particular instant. And, even that is suspect when a second later, life moves on and the moment we just owned is no longer ours. It now belongs to history, and history belongs to those who wish to control you.

My assignment is absurd. I'm writing this and it may all change. Daffodil may die in my past. I may be forced to write I never met the woman I love as our lives together fade from my memory. I may yet be forced to write her untimely death, while somewhere she is still asleep in our bed, and then with a blink no longer will be. Do you see? Please, for my sake, just nod your head and keep reading so I'm not losing my mind for no reason.

Have you ever been in love? I hope so. Do you know the coldness of being taken away from the only thing that makes you want to breathe everyday? I hope not. If this weren't about her, if she weren't real and waiting for me somewhere, then existence be damned. I would not be writing this stupid fucking book that is supposed to save the universe.

Oh fuck it.

I've begun smashing clocks. Frustration turns into anger and the only things I have to hurt are these Bobdamned clocks and myself.

The clocks have faces and arms but no feeling, and still, smashing them provides a brief sense of vindication. Honestly, a fleeting sense of freedom from tyranny as well. Of course, as soon as I've smashed one my anger and resentment turn to remorse and woefulness. I'm selfish. Lamenting my personal strife while the universe hangs in the balance? What a prick. I should be doing my job, and with joy for that matter. Instead I'm sad again. Lonely again. I'll be damned…if I'm not already.

Why Bob, why?

To get me the right truck.

To get me the right truck?

Sorry. I dozed off. Petulance is exhausting. I just woke up and read that last thing I wrote. What a child. I'm angry with Bob, sure. Suppose I've always been, though I know it's not her fault. Thank Bob that Bob has a sense of humor.

She really does. She likes to turn phrases using her name, like we do. Only, because it's her name she replaces God or Bob with "me" and thinks it's hilarious every time. I asked her once if she thought there was anyone or anything that could save humanity from itself. Her answer: "Me I hope not."

But perhaps her favorite joke, already witnessed by you just a few paragraphs ago, is her answer to the almighty question, "Why Bob, why?" Her favorite answer, every hilarious fucking time, is: "To get you the right truck."

Rocking sense of humor or not, it is her fault you know? She started all this shit. Sigh.

I typed that sigh because I sighed super hard right then. Seriously. Alliteration aside, that shit was real. But let's move on. Perhaps a joke? What makes a woodpecker peck?

Maybe I should just get back to the story.

22

I suppose now is as good a time as any to start explaining how Bobby Gout wound up in an alternate dimension located inside a young woman's mind, chasing a cosmic entity named Timmy who's bent on the destruction of our universe. How Timmy battled with Bobby's brother, Curtis Gout, and trapped his soul in a jigsaw puzzle. How Timmy also battled The King of Shar-Crypt-On for his special key. How Mr. Brownstone ran away with that key. And who is this Mr. Brownstone fella I've just mentioned for the first time?

Don't fret, I'm going to dump some much needed background information on you. Well deserved too, if you've stuck with me this far. A few chapters of boring details and then we'll get back to Daffodil, I promise. Hopefully, she's the one you're the most concerned with.

Let's go back and visit Bobby Gout first. Bobby murdered his former employer, a giant of a Chinaman named Gladys, then ran away with several hundred thousand dollars. Bobby didn't want the money. He killed for love. The money was taken in an effort to escape. Gladys was only a piece of the criminal organization Bobby had betrayed and not its only power-player. Bobby knew they would come looking for him.

Truthfully, I think Bobby wanted to be found, whether he will admit that or not. The loss of Cilia had left him heartbroken. The type of heartbreak that tricks a person into thinking they want their own life to end. Telltale sign I'm correct? He could have ran off without stealing the money. Stealing the money sealed his fate, although as you shall soon discover, not in the manner expected.

The squadron of goons found Bobby quickly, and off to the desert they went. What a convenient arena for disappearing bodies, the desert. Lakes and rivers are nice but you never hear about a dead body from the desert suddenly washing ashore to reopen a missing person's investigation. Nope. The desert is Earth's most solemn burial ground for illegally disposed of corpses. The desert takes its job seriously. So much so, it refuses adherence to concepts of time and location within its borders. In the desert, it's all the same fucking day (or night) and the same fucking place. In this instance, somewhere between Los Angeles and Las Vegas. Ostensibly, the middle of nowhere.

A full moon presided over the impending fulfillment of Bobby's death sentence. He'd already dug his own grave. From behind him, the headlights of a car glinted off the barrel of a gun as it moved into position, muzzled against the back of Bobby's head. He heard a click, the readying of the gun to fire. This was the end. Bobby's teeth were clinched with the lock-jawed resignation of fate. He stared intently into the darkness of night, waiting for the flash of light, the pop, and then the flash of life before his eyes. Instead, he heard a second click?

The headlights of the car glinted off the barrel of a second, much larger gun, buried in the nape of the man holding the pistol pointed at Bobby. "You boys put all those hammers to the ground. Throw 'em over there to the side or I'm gonna get started with this fella, work my way through the rest of you."

Bobby didn't recognize the voice at all, not even a hint.

"Alright, everybody into the hole."

The men climbed down into the hole Bobby dug for himself. They stood there together, arms raised, looking very angry about the fact that only moments before they were going to get to kill somebody, and now they were probably going to get killed instead. If not by this mysterious jerk then by their bosses. Life is so unfair.

Bobby took the gun at the back of his head from the hands of a man named Charlie Dink, who everybody called The Dink. He pistol-whipped The Dink out of spite. The Dink collapsed into the hole with the rest of his associates. He muttered foul words for foul occasions such as these, lacing Bobby and the stranger with insolent promises of their impending demise at his hands. Pretty standard, rather unimaginative threats to be honest. The Dink.

"Who the hell are you?" Bobby can't see the man's face. Only a silhouette illuminated by the car's headlights. The man was tall. He stood with the posture of an Old-West gunfighter.

"Don't matter. Just come with me if you want to live."

"Don't want to live."

"Well, come with me anyways."

Bobby opened his mouth again, lungs filled with more questions he was not allowed to ask.

"Come on dummy. I'm saving your worthless life." The man turned and trotted off into the darkness. Bobby shut his mouth and followed. Instinct.

The men in the pit, guns no longer pointed in their direction, clambered out of the hole and went after their own weapons. Then after Bobby and the stranger. Gunshots rang through the desert air. In between the sounds of his own panting, the reports from the gunfire echoed in Bobby's ears. He ran blindly in the direction of the stranger. In between the gunshots, he could hear his former associates behind him as they bellowed promises of pain and death for both he and his anonymous savior. Eventually, Bobby spotted a dim light ahead.

The two men sped down a desert highway, direction unknown. The stranger was behind the wheel. Bobby was silent. Both pointed a gun at the other.

In their fury, the hoodlums gave chase on foot. Each of them thought someone else would bring the car. Truly, sometimes goodness's only saving grace is the stupidity cultivated in the anger of badness.

By the time they returned to their cars, the villains realized the chase was over. They would tell their bosses Bobby was dead and buried in the desert, then keep the money Bobby had left behind and split it amongst themselves. Their cover story would claim that Bobby had locked the money in a locker somewhere and swallowed the key before they could stop him. For an extra thousand bucks, one particularly greedy idiot sacrificed the tip of a finger, supposedly bitten off by Bobby during a struggle to prevent him from swallowing the key, thus legitimizing their lies. That was that. Don't worry. They all eventually got what they deserved.

"How did you know we were out there?" Bobby asked.

"I could see the lights from the highway," the stranger replied.

Bobby scoffed at the obvious lie. "Why did you help me?"

"What difference does it make? Redemption. How's that? Who cares?"

"Who are you?"

"Nobody. Your guardian angel. What's it matter? A thousand other bullshit answers. We won't be seeing each other again after tonight. My job's not to explain shit to you. My job was getting you out."

Of course none of the stranger's answers suited Bobby, but this is the way conversations may go between two strangers pointing weapons at one another. Indeed, you might find yourself much more respectful of another person's privacy if they are aiming a firearm at you. Or, if you're dying, you may just not give a shit to answer questions from the dickhead who just got you shot.

"Well do you mind if I at least know where we're going?"

"You're going someplace safe. I'm not going anywhere 'cept in the dirt." The man pulled the car over to the side of the rode and turned on the interior lights. His shirt was saturated in blood down near his stomach. "I'm gut shot. Those idiots managed to hit me back there."

"Fuck. I'm sorry. I…"

"Just shut up and listen close to me. There's a place I was headed. Was taking you. You need to go there. You have to. Trust me. You need to see what's there, but you're gonna have to do it on your own now." Blood trickled from his mouth as he spoke, but he managed to tell Bobby what he was supposed to look for, where he was supposed to go.

"I don't understand. Why did you do this?"

"The universe is giving you a second chance Bobby Gout. I suggest you take it." The man smiled a bloody smile and died. Bobby had never told him his name.

Back then, Bobby Gout believed the man was his guardian angel. In a way, he was, if only for a particular moment in time. The man's name was Jacob Trate and he was the twelfth generation of Trate men that descended from my adopted son, Daniel. Jacob was also my childhood friend. Figure that out.

Jacob Trate sent Bobby Gout looking for an old filling station. I'm not sure where Bobby found the station because it moves. I once found it in Virginia, I think.

The filling station wasn't really a filling station, though gas would have flowed from the pumps if needed, and at a very reasonable price. The front of the building looked well enough like a highway store, but inside was a house full of books and food. There wasn't even an office, although there was an old cash register positioned just inside the front door next to a coat rack. The cash register was resting on what had once been a sewing table and there was eighty-six cents in the drawer.

Bobby hid at the station for months before he finally discovered its big secret. Perhaps the more accurate statement would be, before the station's big secret revealed itself. He was out behind the building gathering wood when he noticed the shimmering, floating, cloud looking thing. Bobby was certain the object had not been there before. Certain. He'd been out back almost daily and that thing was not there before.

But, maybe it was?

Was it?

Sure it was. He'd been pondering whether or not he should stick his head into the cloud looking thing all this time, to see what was in there. Yeah. Every day he'd been pondering this situation. Right? Since the day he arrived. Yes. He'd been weighing the pros and cons, and had decided he was going to jump in. That's right. He remembered this all made sense. Why had he even thought there for a second he'd never seen the thing before? That was crazy. What was he waiting for? Bobby shrugged his shoulders with a roll of his eyes, shook his head with an incredulous smile, and entered the portal.

23

Curtis Gout was built with a different sort of tenacity than his brother Bobby, and was a different type of adventurer. Born and raised in the "not quite the Confederate south, but definitely a notch on the Bible Belt" city of Louisville, Kentucky, Curtis hadn't strayed far from home for most of his life. His only substantial travels outside his hometown were to boxing rings throughout Chicago, where he relocated as an adult to take regular beatings from men who were much more talented and well trained than him. He made a good living taking punches, and though he lost more than a few of his teeth, he never got knocked out. Curtis was known throughout Chicago as the best sparring partner an up-and-coming talent could work with. No one could take a punch like Curtis Gout.

Curtis was genuinely perplexed when he received the written telegram from his brother. The message was odd. For one thing, Bobby was out in the middle of nowhere all by his self. This didn't sound like his brother. For thing number two, Bobby sent a telegram. Telegrams weren't often sent anymore. The strange circumstances made Curtis wonder if Bobby was doing drugs. Thus, inspired by familial love and frightened curiosity, Curtis heeded the call of the message and set out to find his brother.

When Curtis finally arrived at the filling station, his brother was gone. He found a handwritten note from Bobby, his brother's old watch, and the wisdom of ages trapped in the pages of all the books stacked throughout the station. Oh, there was also that strange floating thingy out back behind the building. There was also that.

Months of waiting for his brother to return passed before Curtis decided to enter the portal. Despite the note Bobby had left explaining his use of the portal and ensuring he would return, Curtis lost his patience. Bobby was taking too long. Curtis feared his brother was in peril so he said, "Ah, tuh hell with it," and jumped on in.

For some odd reason the portal spit him out on the front porch of the filling station. Again and again he jumped in, but the damn thing just kept spitting Curtis back out on the front porch. Eventually he accepted there was a reason this was happening, though he still took several more leaps through the portal out of spite for the situation.

On his last jump – he'd promised himself it was the last time he would succumb to his compulsion – when he woke up back on the front porch there was another note from his brother. As it turned out, Bobby was at least still alive, as the note very distinctively said: I'm Alive.

That was all. "I'm Alive." Curtis had a right-hook to the body lined up for the next time he saw his little brother. "I'm Alive." The little shit. There couldn't possibly have been enough time to write a

little more information into that note, could there have been? Jackass.

While Curtis waited for Bobby to return he read away his boredom.
As I mentioned before, the books that filled the rooms of the filling
station held much of the wisdom of the universe. Scholarship took
root in Curtis. Along the way he learned to meditate, he exercised,
and he did chores around the house. Over time, he built a long
hallway from the house to the portal and a small room (whose
exterior looked like a tool shed) around the portal itself. All these
things he did while waiting for his brother to return, but Bobby
would not come back, for despite Bobby's previous written assur-
ances, his return was not part of Bob's plan.

The more Curtis read the more he began to realize his soul
twisted in the hands of fates considerably more powerful than his
personal will. His life was not his own. Yet, he found peace within
the chaos, and the universe revealed itself to him. The histories of
countless centuries, of countless worlds and lives, countless cultures
of forgotten names and locations, the words and ideas and emotions
of each and every soul to have ever existed, all were forever en-
grained in the DNA of our universe. Those are the words that lined
the shelves of that special place.

There was a copy of this book on one of the shelves as well. I over-
looked it when I was there. Curtis opened it once, but at the time
these pages were blank. This was not the only book at the filling

station with empty pages, waiting to be written. Existence happens fast. Bob's writing assignments are often backlogged.

With the passage of time, Curtis realized his purpose at the station. Exercising intense concern and effort he learned to control the portals, and through meditation he began to have visions of his brother. Bobby was on some form of mission, searching for something and somehow running from that same thing all at once. A force that Curtis couldn't see but could feel. As you know, that force was the monster, Timmy. Curtis sensed its anger and insanity, and all the pain and anguish the evil being was creating. He could hear "people" in agony. As Timmy's power grew, Curtis felt its bitterness spreading throughout the universe.

With great effort, Curtis began to help his brother, sending portals to Bobby while he chased Timmy through time and space. Through all levels of existence. Infinite timelines of infinite dimensions. Curtis and Bobby fought Timmy together, pieces falling into their places, but the universe was losing time. Timmy was growing stronger every moment, Bob was growing older, and the brothers Gout were only human – at least back then.

Somewhere along the way I got involved. I was adrift, or so I thought when I was young, and happened upon Curtis while walking in the summer rain. A beautiful day, I remember. He would not say so the day we met, but Curtis had expected me. I was part of Bob's plan, another piece of the puzzle, and now here I stand naked, stripped of all the desperate illusions we call reality, sewn together and worn as armor for our sanity.

24

Mr. Brownstone was the last of his kind, for the time being. From a race of asexual shape-shifters, his home planet, Kilotilla, was previously known as the most uncomfortable place in the universe. Kilotilla was one of the first planets destroyed by Timmy. Uncomfortable or not, Kilotilla and its inhabitants did not deserve annihilation.

The King of Shar-Crypt-On investigated the destruction of the planet. He'd never seen anything like it. For lack of better words, the planet and all its lifeforms "rotted" at an accelerated rate. What we now know is that Timmy burrowed deep inside Kilotilla's core, where he drained the entire unified organism of planet and surface level creatures of their life-force.

The King, unable to stop the decomposition of life on Kilotilla, rescued a single newborn child from the destruction before the child succumbed to Timmy's evil. The King named the child Mr. Jerry Brownstone and raised Jerry as his own. Eventually, Mr. Brownstone would become The King's Chief of Security and personal bodyguard.

The reason Kilotilla, prior to it's destruction, was known as the most uncomfortable place in the universe? The Kilotillans' ability to shape-shift. What's so uncomfortable about shapeshifters you may ask, if you've never been around one? It's intimidating as hell, that's what. If you've ever been in the presence of rare talent, you should understand. Anyone assigned to mediocrity (or worse) by the big-roulette-wheel-of-cosmic-fates would have a hard time not being jealous, or if not jealous than at least self-conscious, and therefor, uncomfortable. Sure, this might be some pathetic form of self-loathing egocentrism on the part of us "normies," but I'm telling you, even if they're super nice, you just don't want to be alone in a room full of shape-shifters.

Mr. Brownstone, however, is our friend, and right now, somewhere in time, he's desperately on the run for the universe's life.

One last particular item of note in regards to Mr. Brownstone's species: A Kilotillan's shapeshifting ability is limited to one alternate form. So, that fact revealed, guess what non-humanoid shape Mr. Brownstone can take. Correct. A ferret. A ferret somewhere lost in time, running around an alternate dimension inside my wife's teenage mind. A ferret carrying the very key to our existence, along with a significant amount of emotional stress.

You see, Mr. Brownstone, while deeply concerned for the universe, is equally concerned with the propagation of his species. That's right folks, Mr. Brownstone is pregnant. He's reached the birthing age of his people and will soon bring forth the first newborn Kilotillan in more than, well I'm not sure exactly how long, but it's been a long while.

Can you imagine? Most people would protect their child at all costs. This guy has the singular responsibility of keeping his entire species alive and that item is number two on his list of priorities! Obviously, safely delivering his child will mean nothing if Timmy destroys the entirety of existence.

Still, at night when he has the chance to sleep, Mr. Brownstone dreams of the baby. The harrowing burden of his mission slips away as his mind plays fancy with parenthood. He dreams of a healthy birth for his child. Of the first words spoken. Of the first steps taken. Of that most significant day in a Kilotillan's life, the Day of First Change. He hopes his child will change shapes into something useful and fun and self-gratifying. Like any good parent, Mr. Brownstone is deeply concerned with his unborn child's future self-esteem.

I know this was awfully late to introduce a new player, but I told you I don't know what I'm doing. Besides, technically Mr. Brownstone has been here the whole time. You just didn't know who the ferret was and I didn't know when to discuss his origin story with you. I may move this passage to earlier in the book during edits. Right now I'm running out of time and things must be said. Things must be done.

I've smashed another clock. My patience is thin. Being trapped in this place, with the history of existence unfolded before me as one single moment, it's dizzying. Exhausting.

I'm tired, but we have a universe to save. Maybe you should help. Honestly we could use all the help we can get. Daffodil, Curtis,

Bobby, The King, Mr. Brownstone. Me. We can't do this on our own. Perhaps by the end of this story I'll have written your name, and you'll be a hero as well. Or maybe I'll just fuck off instead.

25

This is an abnormally long chapter. Potentially ponderous. Don't worry, we'll take some breaks but you should definitely have some nachos and beer handy.

When Robert Alexander Gout first went through the portal, he found himself in the midst of a war on the planet Shar-Crypt-On. He landed in a village as everyone was arming themselves against an attack. Everything happened so fast he only had time (time… time…time…) to ask a few questions. Action-adventure questions like, "Where am I?" and "Why are you fighting?" along with, "Where can a guy get a good cheeseburger around here?"

It was a grand uprising he was told. There was a usurper infecting the planet's harmony, a princess in distress, and an army of souls possessing weak wills and ill-mannered dispositions who needed a spanking. Bobby joined the fight on impulse. As the village was invaded, Bobby looked across the lines of battle and saw a familiar set of eyes relocated on a new body.

You see, after Bobby killed Gladys on Earth, Timmy's consciousness was dispersed throughout the universe. His evil, emboldened, spread. Much like our concept of Satan on Earth, Timmy's will had infected those with weak hearts on many planets. The warrior Bobby faced on the battlefront of Shar-Crypt-On was not actually the physical Timmy, simply one of the monster's possessions.

Bobby fought many battles during that war but held to one promise he'd made with himself. Never take another life (except Timmy's, if given the opportunity). This may seem ridiculous for a hero in the middle of a war but it was a solemn oath, and one to which he remained committed. He showed as much mercy as fierceness in defeating The King's enemies. Unfortunately, it was this same mercy that led to the death of The King's daughter, whom Bobby had given his heart. Though his quiet integrity was the driving force behind the end of the civil war on Shar-Crypt-On, Bobby had lost another love. Yet, (and although no remedy to the anguish of a broken heart…) Bobby had earned the honor and respect of The King.

As I told you before, The King was no ordinary soul. Though he was in aguish with the loss of his daughter, certainly, he knew someday he would see her again. He also knew he'd found something special in Bobby Gout. Bobby's compassion and grace during battle made him a true hero, so The King selected him for a new mission.

Here was the assignment: Bobby was to travel the universe rescuing children. Timmy was destroying planets at an ever increasing rate, gaining strength, power, and knowledge. Bobby was tasked with making sure he outpaced Timmy, preventing the monster from completely destroying entire race's of sentient life, just as The King had rescued Mr. Brownstone. Although Bobby's true desire was to confront the monster, he accepted The King's mission. Bobby would gather as many children as possible and return them to The King for protection. For as long as at least one soul from each civilization remained, the goodness the universe had endowed in each of those planets would survive and Timmy would never be truly victorious.

The King had an extensive team of scientists running around rescuing and cataloguing plants and animals as well. And Bobby wasn't The King's only soldier rescuing children. However, due to the apparent uniqueness of Bobby's soul, he was the only soldier The King placed directly in the path of Timmy, rescuing children from planets in the midst of their destruction.

As mentioned before, Curtis Gout learned to control the portals and was able to assist Bobby on his rescue mission. The unhappy reality of this situation is that Curtis never fully understood his brother's mission. His visions of Bobby were flashes of mental images and emotions, only partially clear, and shadowed by the darkness of Timmy's presence. The one thing he understood was if he was going to help his brother, his only way to do so was with the portals. Thus, with Bob's will, Curtis sent portals to move Bobby from planet to planet while Bobby gathered the kids.

Meanwhile, not only did Curtis send the portals to his brother, he also used them on Timmy. Whenever Timmy got dangerously close to Bobby, Curtis would send a portal to intercept him. This helped keep the monster off Bobby's trail, but also sent Timmy to his next destination, ultimately dooming a planet. Of course, Bobby would then get sent to rescue children from whatever planet Curtis had unfortunately sent the monster to devour. Talk about vicious cycles.

Actively participating in the doom of so many distant planets and creatures was extraordinarily painful for Curtis. Curtis understood he was damning new planets when he used the portals on Timmy to protect Bobby, and on more than one occasion, in effort to save Bobby's life, Curtis unknowingly and unintentionally forced Bobby to leave behind children he was meant to rescue, which devastated Bobby, and in turn, sensing his brother's pain, Curtis. The yin to the cosmic yang was that Curtis' assistance also allowed Bobby to save more children than would have otherwise ever been possible. Such is life.

Another mark of a true hero for you to add to your list: Empathy. As you now understand, for every child Bobby saved, thousands, if not millions, if not billions were left behind to die. His heart was constantly torn between what good he could do and that which he could not. He likened this pain to the rotting destruction those left behind souls were suffering as their planets and lives were consumed. His reality was agonizing. Why was he chosen to live, to survive this insanity? Bobby felt he deserved the same fate of all those he was forced to leave behind, but he moved forward, doing what good he could.

Timmy hunted, the universe burned, and Bobby yearned for the day when he might finally have the opportunity to confront the monster head on. Perhaps when the time came, Bob would see fit to let Bobby die with honor and take that bastard cosmic fuck Timmy with him. Bobby would have gladly burned in Hell for eternity as long as Timmy was in the cage next to him.

We have one choice for cosmic survival. One choice between two available options: Choose silliness and smile, or choose pragmatic realism and drown in the deeply morose emotional landscape that is existence. In that regard, the most important thing Bob ever told me was, "You have got to find joy and keep it in your life."

Of course, I, being human and therefor misunderstanding most of what she tries to tell us heard, "There is a woman named Joy you must make your wife." I looked at Bob confused, knowing that she knew I was already married and desperately in love. Bob laughed her head off then told me to pull her finger.

Bob chose infinite silliness a long time ago. And fart jokes. Bob loves fart jokes. She really is a weirdo.

It was silliness, the infinite reasons to laugh, that kept Bobby Gout sane during his journey. For instance, the first part of Bobby's trip is a little adventure I like to call: Traversing the Deconstruction. The Deconstruction was a series of planets on which Bob experimented in an effort to better understand humans. She created entire planets with races of people that were only endowed with specific traits of human nature. Once her research on a planet was finished, she would allow those planets to evolve into whole species. However, the affects of the Deconstruction remained, creating a hilarious set of circumstances that shaped these species' emotional evolution.

Bobby got a lot of comedic mileage out of these planets. Unfortunately, Bobby wasn't a comedian.

Most of the planets on Bobby's journey were "normal." Just your average societies, piddling along on their paths to eventual destruction, completely oblivious that said destruction was actually about to happen. Timmy was coming and hell was riding the pale horse behind him. Or something like that.

Anyway, during his mission there were two planets that Bobby wound up on by accident. They weren't part of his children saving trip itinerary, but sometimes the portals didn't quite work correctly. The second planet Bobby landed on by accident was called Liefizard. On Liefizard there is one wealthy man who lives in opulence on a large hill above everyone else. The rest of the planet is poor as dirt.

The man of wealth is a philosopher and writer, and very concerned with the plight of his *lesser* brethren. He has two current publications widely circulated throughout several universes. The first, *The Fraudulent Nature of Sentient Beings*, is an exercise in self-contempt. The book expresses the sadness of his burden, his contempt for the responsibility cast upon him and how that sense of responsibility is utter bullshit, thus making him an utterly fraudulent and loathsome creature. Yet in his follow up work, *The Cosmic Train of Things*, he forgives himself through the mantra of fate, recklessly explaining away the nature of existence with the stroke of a pen while continuing to keep all the damn money on his planet. The rich man's current work in progress is a treatise on the working class's responsibility for their own economic plight. It takes into account the very real systemic oppression instituted long before he was born, and lays the groundwork to a path forward that will see all of the poor folk rise above the horribly unfortunate life circumstances Bob thrust upon them. The working title is *Why Bob Why?*

Anyway, the rich guy's a good dude and he earnestly cares about the poor, but I don't understand why he doesn't just give every one else some damn money. He could give away most of it and still be extremely well-off. So, despite his genuine, super sincere concern for the poor folk, and despite his admittedly well-written books, the poor folk think he is a big fat douche. In fact, the Secret Poor Man's Planetary Motto is enormously long, ever growing, and does nothing but exercise contempt for the rich man. Here's an excerpt:

No matter what the rich man does he will never understand the plight of the poor. Even if he were to give away all his possessions, he would have the self-satisfaction of doing so, something those with nothing will never taste. If the rich man were forced into poverty, he would still have the memory of his better life, something the poor man will never see. Therefore, no matter what, the poor man will always be worse off than the rich man, no matter what, and he will always have a right to say so. Unless the poor man becomes rich. Then he will simply be another rich prick.

Sorry. I wandered a bit and wound up ahead of myself. The point of this is that Bobby Gout royally screwed up on Liefizard. We'll get back to that before too long. First…

The first planet Bobby wound up on by accident was a nameless frozen tundra. There were only two sentient creatures living there, and they were a couple of serious underachievers. I really have no idea what Bob was doing with them, but who says Bob has to have a purpose in everything? People think she does, but Bob has never come right out and said that to me so I think the whole idea is suspect. Maybe she just liked these two dudes so much she dropped them in their own little Utopia, like Heaven, only all by themselves and not yet dead.

Either way, these two goofballs were living in a tiny little shack. There was an endless supply of food and beer. They never questioned the source or why everything they ate and drank each day replenished miraculously. They may not have been too smart but I never met them personally so I can't say. Perhaps they were simply wise enough not to question an endless supply of food and beer. Perhaps they were on a mission, just as Bobby was, and just as I am, but much less bitchy about their assignment.

Bobby suddenly appeared. The two Dudes seemed unsurprised. "Whoa," said Dude Number 1, with little excitement in his voice.

"Sweet," said Dude Number 2.

"Where am I?" asked Bobby Gout.

"Don't know," replied Dude 1.

"*Punch-Out*?" asked Dude 2.

"Excuse me?" said Bobby.

"*Punch-Out* bro'. Grab the sticks," said Dude 1.

All these idiots had to entertain themselves was a busted old television and an original Nintendo Entertainment System with *Mike Tyson's Punch-Out*. It was their only form of activity besides eating, drinking, shitting, and sleeping.

"Are there any children here?" asked Bobby.

"No dude, it's just the two of us on the whole freaking planet," replied Dude 1.

"Are you sure?" asked Bobby.

"Yeah dude, we're sure," replied Dude 2. "Someone would have found us by now."

Bobby was about to argue that giant leap in logic when a new portal opened. He assumed this meant the dudes were correct and he was on the wrong planet. Unfortunately, just as he was about to jump back through his portal, one of those damn fool dude's uttered the words, "Damn! We can never beat that fucker."

Mike Tyson's Punch-Out was a flashback to the simpler times of Bobby's childhood, and one of his all time favorite video games. Bobby turned away from the portal, picked up the controller, and proceeded to whip Mike Tyson's ass. It was an absolute blast and he played for hours. He must have broke his own high score on four or five occasions.

For a short time, Bobby was relieved of his burdens and mentally transported to a state of frivolous contentment. The problem was, he was on a mission and wasting time, time that didn't belong to him. Whipping Mike Tyson's ass in a video game was not part of Bob's plan. Or was it? Either way, two of the children on Bobby's list died. His selfish desire to forget for a moment that he was operating with a purpose had killed them. Later, when The King explained to him what he'd done, Bobby wept as the names of those two children faded from his list. Lesson learned.

By the way, as far as I know those two dudes are still sitting there playing *Punch-Out* and wasting enough time for the entire universe. Dear Bob I wish I knew their purpose.

I first met Curtis Gout during Bobby's rescue mission. I wandered upon the filling station in the rain and Curtis took me in. I was sixteen years old. I had taken up a quest, wandering by foot on a search for peace and discovery. I discovered some shit. Yes sir. That is for s...u...r...e, certain.

I remember Curtis standing there on the front porch, spitting with the wind. He was an old fellow when we met. His lack of teeth unnerved me.

"Would you like to come in from the rain?" he asked.

I accepted. Many days were spent together in the filling station. We chatted and played checkers, and Curtis taught me how to box. Then one day he showed me the portal and my adventure into the universe began.

That was the first time I was given the responsibility of saving the universe. I wanted to serve a grand purpose, and I was given one, or so I thought at the time. Now my job doesn't seem so special. I have saved the universe a total of thirty-two times in my life, on a daily basis during stretches, and my assignments are often absurd.

For instance, once, I received a phone call in the middle of the night. My assignment was to find the first vending machine I could and buy an orange soda. Whalla! The universe was saved.

Once, I received a telegram requesting my presence at an auction. I purchased a very old violin that would no longer play in tune, then smash it to bits. Again, universe saved. Thank Bob!

Once, I was sent to a local steakhouse to eat an entire sixty-four ounce steak without vomiting. Zazoo! Universe saved.

These little episodes got more inane. More Bobdamned ridiculous. I was beginning to believe the universe was fucking with me. Of course, that was before I met Bob. Before I was taught all that I've learned in this tiny, lonely little room. Now I'm certain the universe is fucking with me.

Anyway, the day before I arrived here I received an anonymous letter in the mail. This is what the letter read:

Write a book. Tell the truth. Finish the story. Save the universe.

I went to sleep that night lying next to Daffodil. I woke up here. Now you know what's really going on. Frankly, the entire situation is beginning to piss me off. Fuck that, it's already pissed me off. The only good to ever come out of any of this bullshit for me, is her. You see, on that first mission, the first time I saved the universe, what I really saved was a person. My wife. And she saved me right back.

We have reached the beginning of the end of Curtis Gout's mortal life. His death occurs during Bobby's quest to save the children, after I left Curtis at the filling station for my own mission. His demise began with a nightmare.

Curtis was dreaming of his brother and the monster. Something was wrong. He could feel it in his feet, and when he woke in his easy chair the uneasy feeling remained. Curtis had somehow placed Bobby in peril.

Curtis realized that while sleeping, through his dreams, he'd accidentally sent out portals that brought Timmy and Bobby together on the same planet. This was when Bobby made his unfortunate error in judgment on the planet Liefizard. Suddenly afforded the opportunity to confront the monster, Bobby abandoned his rescue mission for a battle, a battle for which he was not prepared.

Curtis sat in the station watching the scene unfold in his mind's eye. Sweat and confusion poured from his body. He sent another portal to his brother, and another, and another, encouraging his escape.

Bobby refused. His rage for the evil creature was relentless. He fought courageously, but no weapon Bobby was equipped with had been designed for the destruction of a cosmic being. Eventually, Bobby fell and faced death. Timmy's hand rose to strike its fatal blow when Curtis did the only thing he could think of to save his little brother's life. Curtis opened a portal in front of himself, reached in, and pulled the monster through. There was a flash of light, then darkness.

Curtis opened his eyes to find he was still in his reading chair in the filling station. His skin tingled and rose in bumps. The hair stood up on his entire body and a breeze of dark air hushed past him. Curtis closed his eyes and breathed deeply. When he opened them again, Timmy sat across the room on a couch. The creature had taken the form of Curtis' mother and was smiling wickedly.

"Care for a glass uh lemonade?" was all Curtis could think to say. He was terrified.

Timmy's ability to create fear and intimidate, along with his unnatural strength and power, were institutes of nature. As I've mentioned before, Timmy was an idiot. His brain was a vault filled with infinite knowledge he had no understanding for. Imagine a computer filled with data but without an operating system powerful enough to utilize the information. The monster's tyrannical success had come in spite of complete intellectual ineptitude, but at the time, no one knew what a fool the evil monster truly was.

"What is lemonade?" Timmy responded.

Curtis was unnerved by the perfect replication of his mother's voice. "It's a drink." Curtis' voice was shaky. "It tastes good."

"I'm going to eat you," said his mother.

"Well then you'll need somethin to wash me down with." Curtis smiled as he gained his bearings. Curtis Gout had been ready to die long before he followed his brother's letter to the filling station. Mortality was a concept he had accepted at a young age. A concept deeply intertwined with his career as a boxer. Curtis reminded himself of that fact, then felt the tension in his body ease. He rose to go to the kitchen. Timmy started from the couch. "Stay still," said Curtis. "Whereya think I'ma run off to?"

"You brought me here," said his mother. "You have power."

"Maybe a little. I'm justa man though." Curtis turned and fetched the lemonade. His mind raced as he walked. He knew he was about to die but that wasn't what plagued him. These are the thoughts that flooded his personal airwaves: How could he make his death mean something? How would Bobby move forward? What would happen to the portals? Would Timmy gain control of them? Could he kill it?

Curtis returned with the lemonade on a tray and a large caliber handgun tucked into the back of his trousers. He had little hope in the weapon but he figured, "*what the hell?*" Months earlier he would never have believed anything he'd witnessed at the filling station. Maybe the Good Lord would intervene.

"Why ya so angry?" asked Curtis.

"I do not like this drink," said his mother. "It is sour."

"It's s'posed to be," Curtis said. The monster took another sample taste and Curtis changed the subject. "I'm curious, whatcha trying to do here?"

"I'm going to swallow your soul," she hissed with a curl of her lip. "They taste…good."

Though he was frightened, an unexpected benefit happened in the presence of Timmy. Curtis could "see" his brother with his eyes wide open, no meditation required. Bobby had managed to return safely to Shar-Crypt-On and was recovering from his wounds. In Bobby's timeline several weeks had already passed since his fight with the monster. Still, he was going to need more time to heal before he could continue his mission.

"Would ya like to hear uh story?" asked Curtis. The best thing he could do was keep Timmy distracted as long as possible. The longer he could keep the monster at the filling station, the better off the universe would be.

The next five months of human time were spent with the freaky doppelganger of his mother. Ick! Five months alone in confined quarters with your real mother would be bad enough. But five months with a monster, knowing at some point it is going to lose its temper and eat you? Swallow your very soul!

I have to admit, I think Curtis had already gone a little nutso. He kept the absurd villain occupied with stories and interesting conversation for as long as possible and managed to have a little fun at the monster's expense along the way. Albeit very nervous fun.

When it became clear to him that Timmy was still a mental child, Curtis realized he might be able to slow the monster's progress by filling its head with nonsense and lies. He stroked the loon's ego with hopes of encouraging the folly of false confidence. But ever so often, unintentionally, the monster would do something that made Curtis feel like he was really sitting with his mother. This would briefly make Curtis feel guilty for all the lies and chicanery.

One day the unavoidable finally happened. Like a child the monster lost its patience. Curtis had just finished a very long version of his favorite fairy tale, Hop-o'-My-Thumb, by Charles Perrault. Timmy wanted to hear another. Curtis refused. It was time for bed, simple as that. Timmy smacked Curtis across the room.

"I don't want to sleep. I want another story! You always do this. I hate you." Timmy seethed. "I am tired of this place. I will eat you now, and then I will eat your planet." Ever seen a two year old throw a tantrum? Timmy ran around the room stomping his feet. He grabbed breakables to smash, made sure Curtis was watching, then insolently slammed the items to the floor.

To be frank, Curtis had grown exhausted with his efforts to keep Timmy at the filling station. There's only so much nonsense a man can take. Thus, Curtis pulled out his revolver and shot Timmy in the forehead. What the hell? Maybe the universe would endow the revolver with magic bullets.

A hole the size of a golf ball opened up straight through Timmy's head. Curtis could see the other side of the room in the hole. Timmy smiled and lunged towards Curtis. The old fellow moved swiftly, stepping aside and tripping the creature, sending it sprawling to the floor.

"How could you do that," the monster howled, "to your own mother?" Timmy laughed uproariously then stood and changed forms. He was now an athletic mime in boxing shorts and gloves.

"You picked the wrong sport young man. I know this story well." Curtis confidently punched Timmy in the face. That was the only shot he would get. Timmy's arms began to rotate on their hinges, pummeling Curtis across the room. The monster-mime leapt on top of Curtis and smashed his face inward, crushing his skull.

The pain Curtis Gout felt in that last moment was indescribable. He was my friend. I hate this story.

I'm a little angry with Bob today. I woke up and all the clocks were repaired. Neatly back in order, yes they were. Of course, I have set about to smash them once again, and I will do it every day. I will thumb my nose while they tick away, broken or not. Bob is a clever creator though, most likely laughing her ass off while I waste more time breaking these fucking clocks.

Damn it!

There is still so much to tell, but I don't want to anymore. I know it's just a bad day. Just a bad day. But someone in my head keeps calling me a weakling and I think it's me. It is me. Damn it, I miss my wife and my children. Do you hear me Bob?

I don't want to do this anymore. Can't I just have a nice quiet life with my wife and family?

Why Bob why?

I don't want the goddamn truck…

Timmy sat atop Curtis' dead body and roared his satisfaction, beating his chest like the proverbial gorilla. His victory was short lived however, as a flash of white-hot light sent him sprawling across the room. From his own human ashes, Curtis Gout arose.

Curtis stared down at his arms and legs. He checked his baby-maker out of habit then noticed his human body still lay on the floor. The sight of his own smooshed in face made him double over to wretch, but what came from his mouth was more white light. He straightened up and wiped his mouth out of habit.

Timmy looked very confused, but his confusion quickly returned to anger. The flesh he was wearing dissolved from his body. He was now dark energy shaped like a man.

Curtis wasn't sure what to do. He thought of heroes from his childhood comics and held his hands out in front of him. Energy surged from them, hammering at Timmy, but the monster was still stronger than Curtis. Despite his ineptitude and lack of understanding, Timmy held the power of many planets and souls within him. The monster fired back at Curtis with his own dark, energetic hatred, blasting Curtis through the wall of the filling station.

Curtis found himself unbound in the vastness of space. Before him floated the filling station, surrounded by unending darkness. His amazement with the situation was quickly replaced by the reality that, though he was no longer human, he was still very badly injured. So, he did the only thing he could think of. He fled. Curtis rocketed across the cosmos like a shooting star on steroids. Timmy followed.

Curtis' ability to control the portals wasn't simply learned. It was a birthright. Destiny, so to speak. He would have never understood this while in human form, but once his soul returned to the cosmos everything became clear. The knowledge of all his lifetimes flooded his conscious, along with his understanding for the clockwork of the universe. Curtis Gout's soul had been in Bob's service for many ages.

He was Agent 13, the keeper of the gateway dimension, those hallways of endless doors I spoke of before. While in human form, it was impossible for Curtis to know the gateway dimension was in his possession. That was the point. The easiest way to keep something safe is not only to keep it hidden from the bad guys, but also from its protectors. The gateway dimension had been hidden on Curtis' human body, disguised as a birthmark on his butt, shaped like a shoe.

As Timmy pursued him, Curtis absorbed all of these thoughts and memories and emotions, trying to figure out what in the hell he was going to do next. One thing was certain, Timmy could not be allowed to find the gateway dimension. That was a direct path to the end of existence.

The monster was hot on his tail. Curtis couldn't outrun the bastard, he couldn't outfight it, and using the portals wasn't working either. The gateways wouldn't close fast enough. Every time he opened one to escape through, Timmy flew through the portal as well. Curtis tried throwing portals open directly in front of the monster, but for some reason they just spit Timmy right back out on Curtis' heels.

Curtis was seriously considering flying straight into a star, hoping Timmy would follow, when he accidentally crashed into a major intersection of the Celestial Soulway. As fate would have it, during the melee, Curtis bumped into an old friend.

The Celestial Soulway, as mentioned earlier, is basically the highway system for souls travelling through space. Souls have to get from one place to the other just like physical creatures. Having organized routes keeps the universe running efficiently.

Remind me to tell you about the Soul Closet sometime. That place is hot.

Anyway, Curtis ran into an old pal he'd spent many lifetimes with. They had battled together as physical beings and once as souls in a great war within the consciousness of the universe. In one life they'd been lovers, but the romance ended so awkwardly they rarely spoke of that era. Curtis' friend was a registered soul, Active Unit 257-A.

257-A was in route to a new body and lifetime. 257-A had actually left the Soul Closet for assignment three cycles earlier, but was repeatedly aborted back onto the Soulway. The universe was having a difficult time assigning 257-A to a human host that was interested in fetal gestation.

Oh the glories of chaos and fate, those lusty romantic concepts whose interminable cosmic love affair proves once and for all, universally, that opposites attract.

257-A hurriedly explained its plight to Curtis, laughing and expressing excitement for running into its old friend. It had so many questions! 257-A heard Curtis was on special assignment or had received a promotion, or something like that, and honestly it just yammered on. For you to get a word in conversationally, when 257-A was excited…well, let's just say entire species have been birthed and aged into extinction while awaiting your turn to speak. Curtis finally told his friend to shut up.

"I need your help," Curtis said. "There's very little time."

"Of course!" 257-A replied. "Anything for you. What is it?"

"I need you to hide something for me." Just as Curtis spoke, Timmy arrived and smashed into him with all his ferocity.

"No!" 257-A shouted. In it's temporal transference preparation state of being, 257-A was no help to Curtis in his fight with Timmy.

"Get out of here!" cried Curtis. In an exhausting effort, he broke from Timmy's grasp and blasted the creature away. He looked back at 257-A and opened a portal for it. "Get out of here and get to a body!"

"But what were you going to give me?"

"You already have it! Now go, and be safe!" With his last remaining strength, Curtis ushered his friend through the portal and safely into its mother's womb on Earth.

Curtis floated in the darkness of space, too weak to continue running. Timmy reappeared and began to consume him. The monster not only drained Curtis of his life force, it also tapped into his conscious, accessing his knowledge and wisdom. Timmy learned of Curtis' control over the portals. He tried to wield their power, but without Curtis' years of practice controlling them, portals began opening in rapid fire succession. Timmy and Curtis bounced through the universe at an alarming rate as Timmy continued to feed off Curtis' soul.

Curtis was near expiration. Yet, just as he was about to have his last thought, countless portals opened simultaneously in every direction. Curtis and Timmy were pulled apart, each sucked into their own cosmic doorway. Just before they were completely separated, Timmy cast one final spell of wickedness on Curtis. Then the portals closed, sending hero and villain to destinations unknown, adrift in a sea of "who knows what will happen next?"

As you may have guessed, the final spell Timmy cast on Curtis, coupled with the convenient timing of Curtis entering an interspatial portal, did indeed trap Curtis inside some old lady's crossword puzzle, where he is in fact still currently trapped, quietly cursing away his predicament.

Now, this is where things get a little tricky. The portal Timmy went through sent him backwards through time to The King. This is when their legendary battle begins. The King had not yet met Bobby Gout or sent him on his mission. He'd also not yet saved the life of Mr. Brownstone. This happens later, in between one of The King's skirmishes with Timmy. We'll catch up to that in a bit, but from this moment forth, Timmy's evil would infect the people of Shar-Crypt-On, eventually causing the civil war that Mr. Bobby Gout would someday fall into.

Don't waste too much energy thinking about this time loop. I told you before, on a certain existential level, everything happens all at once. Leave it at that or you'll drive yourself crazy. When you start fucking around with the inner workings of the universe, sometimes you just have to let shit go.

Fate: 1: The will or principle or determining cause by which things in general are believed to come to be as they are or events happen as they do.
2: An inevitable and often adverse outcome, condition, or end. (*Merriam-Webster*)

Back on Shar-Crypt-On, The King was asleep on his throne. This was a regular occurrence, as The King's diligence for the safekeeping of his planet and the universe led to marathon stints of monitoring existence, which led to quite a few unintended naps when his body gave way to exhaustion.

The King was startled awake by a sudden thud, followed by a startling amount of pain in his royal family jewels. When The King opened his eyes, Timmy was seated in his lap. "Is there something I could help you with my boy?" asked The King.

"I know who you are," said Timmy.

Every planet Timmy consumed had endowed him with knowledge, and The King was well known throughout the universe. The monster typically had no idea what to do with the junk filling up his head, but thoughts would suddenly pop up, with no background information or context for the monster to understand them. When Timmy saw The King, pop, there it was: sudden recognition, and Timmy's silly brain hissed, *This is The King, he has the key.*

And Timmy thought back to himself, *What King? What key?*

And his brain thought, *The Key idiot! The one the five-eyed creature told us about!*

And Timmy thought, *Ohhhhhh, the key. That's the one I want isn't it? What was that five-eyed creatures name again? I liked eating him. He was nice.*

Who cares stupid! Just get it!

What?

The key!

And that's what it was like in the head of the bad guy.

"Are you sure?" asked The King. "I don't think we've met."

"Yes. I know you."

"Then I'm at a disadvantage. And I must admit, I normally prefer to be on a first name basis, and perhaps even have shared a meal, before someone winds up in my lap." The King spoke with a charming smile.

Timmy was slightly disappointed, and embarrassed, and confused. He slid from The King's lap coyly, asserting sexuality he did not actually possess.

This creature is an amalgam of harmless illogic and dangerous hatred, the King mused to himself. The King was a very quick judge of character. *This interaction will probably be both extremely fun and extremely sad. Oh well. Such is life.*

"You know why I am here?" Timmy asked. He was pouting for some reason.

"Do you?" asked The King.

"You have something that I must have. Do you know what that is?"

"No, I'm not certain," said The King. "Could you tell me more clearly?"

At this, Timmy roared at The King with the head of a lion. Timmy expected fear. Instead, The King sat calmly.

"You seem like a sporting fellow," The King said. "Perhaps we should have some fun. Do you like to play games?"

"Yes, we can play. For awhile."

The King was a great warrior. He was a musician and a painter. He was a wizard and a warlock, which are very different things. He was a sporting man, sublimely athletic and graceful. He was also a sage, privy to the thoughts and emotions of others, and otherwise given to intuitions that laid the future before him. The King knew he could never defeat Timmy in the one term that was ultimately necessary – death. Just like Curtis, the best he could do was keep the monster busy for as long as possible and allow Bob's other pieces of the puzzle to fall into place. Yes, The King knew Bob and knew Bob's will would eventually be served. Or not, in which case nothing would matter and we would all be dead anyway.

The King decided to keep the competition simple at first. He challenged Timmy to basic sports and children's games. They played Jacks. They played Hide and Seek. They ran races and saw who could jump the highest. They played Freeze Tag once, which isn't very climactic between only two competitors, though he did trick Timmy into remaining frozen for a solid week. Finally the monster lost his patience and ran off in a huff. This was a pattern that would develop over many years. The King would win a game, Timmy would get mad and quit for a bit, then return for another beating.

The King bested Timmy at jousting. He won at Scrat and Tooliatihoo. He outplayed Timmy at cards, chopped wood faster, and created a more popular line of women's clothing on a little planet called Filpetta.

The competitions were not always civil. There were many times when Timmy became enraged and the battle turned ugly. But The King was a master of spells and incantations, and typically bested the monster on the days that turned nasty as well. A few times the battle turned to actual physical confrontation, and although Timmy was much more powerful than The King, he always played within the rules. This of course meant that Timmy got his ass kicked at Earth boxing, Valtrucian martial arts, and several forms of wrestling that are prevalent in the Conundra Galaxy.

As mentioned previously, ever so often, Timmy would lose poorly and run off somewhere into the universe. The King would eventually discover that when Timmy disappeared, he was off destroying planets and consuming souls. These were difficult times for The King, as he always felt a responsibility to keep the monster close to him to prevent as much destruction as possible. Losing the competitions was much easier on The King emotionally, but in order to keep Timmy engaged he had to present an earnest challenge.

Win a little, lose a little, and continuously measure the monster's emotional bio-meter to prevent it from flying off the rails and eating an entire planet? No problem.

A strange kinship developed between the two. Timmy never destroyed The King, and after leaving would always return for more sport. Timmy's patience would eventually decline however. Somewhere in that miscreant head of his, he began to realize The King was plotting against him. These may be the closest feelings to sadness the monster ever understood, outside of the initial loneliness that drove him to insanity and sent him on his jealous quest for the destruction of Bob.

One day, The King and Timmy were having a competition of spells. This wasn't the first time, but Timmy had learned new wickedness and power. The monster really thought he could beat The King for once and in a sense, he did. Timmy, intentionally yet quite accidentally (in regards to implementation), cast a legitimate spell that took root in The King. Neither knew this at the time. The King won their competition that day, appearing no worse for wear, but Timmy had truly won the battle. This was a turning point.

Sometime later The King looked in a mirror and saw his face was older than he remembered. He was aging much faster than he should have been. Definitely a concerning development, but he trusted in Bob, and his trust never waivered. Everything would work itself out, and in the end, even if it didn't, well, that's sort of the same thing.

26

Okay, we're almost caught back up with the rest of the story. That was a super long flashback chapter, right? I tried to warn you.

Anyway, as time wore on, though the curse Timmy put on The King during their competition of spells had taken deep roots, The King and Timmy's battles continued. During this period, while under the curse of accelerated aging, The King saved Mr. Brownstone's life and raised him as a son. It was also during this time that The King met Bobby Gout and sent him on his mission to save children throughout the universe.

On one particular evening, at a point when The King had grown very old, Timmy surprised The King with a visit. This surprise visit was a fortuitous bounce of the ball for the good guys, as The King had been very upset with himself after he and Timmy's most recent bout. Miscalculated banter had caused Timmy to storm out of the castle in a rage. Surely, another planet and entire species of sentient creatures had suffered the consequences.

The King knew efforts were going poorly for Bob in the battle with Timmy. He was afraid if Timmy got away again, he might die before the monster returned, and The King just didn't know what would happen to the universe without him. This wasn't ego, he just really wanted to know what was going to happen.

Anyway, in the hopes of finally putting an end to Timmy's nonsense, The King challenged the monster to a final game of chess. A very heavy game of chess. If The King won, Timmy agreed to go sit in one of the castle towers for an extremely long time. This was a solid wager for The King. Eternity is, after all, an extremely long time, and fit well within those terms. Timmy didn't know what eternity meant. He did however know that for some reason he wanted the thing around The King's neck. That thing he wanted for some reason, was the key.

Thus, The King wagered the most precious key in the universe. In The King's defense, Timmy had never beaten him at chess. The King had wagered the most precious key in the universe! In his defense, the old-age spell was making The King senile, and he was not aware of this new development. Of course, even if he had been aware he was senile he still would have wagered THE MOST PRECIOUS BOBDAMNED KEY IN THE UNIVERSE, because he was senile.

The King was about to checkmate Timmy. He was literally about to move his Rook from H6 to H3 and place Timmy's king in checkmate, when he fell into a coma. Timmy sat for a time studying The King, wondering what had happened.

Mr. Brownstone entered the game room carrying tea for his father. He quietly placed the tea tray on a table and sounded an alarm. This startled Timmy, who decided it was time to leave. The monster opened a portal and was about to go eat some planet somewhere when his brain spoke up. *Wasn't there something you wanted?* it asked.

I think so. Yes I do. I think there was something I wanted.

The key stupid.

I want that thing around his neck.

That's the key stup... Just go get it you jackass. (Timmy's sub-textual voice was a jerk.)

Timmy stooped to take the key from The King's neck when a portal opened behind him. Out popped Bobby Gout with two children in his arms. I have no idea how old they were or what planet they were from, but those kids were ugly as sin. Ugly, ugly children. Honestly, I know exactly what planet they were from but I'm not going to say. Ugly.

Anyway, Timmy stood with the key dangling from its chain in his hand. Mr. Brownstone stared and Bobby stared, and Timmy stared and somewhere Bob watched. Mr. Brownstone slipped off his shoes.

"Jerry," said Bobby to Mr. Brownstone, discretely nodding at the key in Timmy's hand.

Timmy looked at Bobby and then at Mr. Brownstone. *Why did he say Jerry like that? Who's Jerry? Does he think I'm Jerry? Am I Jerry?*

Mr. Brownstone was slowly removing his left sock. Bobby dropped the kids. One landed on his head but he was fine. Timmy turned towards his portal and began to walk in its direction.

"You wait," Bobby ordered as he took steps – small steps – towards the monster.

Timmy stopped and pointed at himself, checking if Bobby was speaking to him. Mr. Brownstone took off his glasses, put them in his chest pocket, and leapt for the key, all the while holding his left sock in his left hand. Timmy was still looking at Bobby. Mr. Brownstone snatched the key from the monsters hand in a flash and dropped it into the sock he was holding, then dove for the portal. While in mid-air Mr. Brownstone shapeshifted into a ferret. As his clothes dropped loosely to the floor, Mr. Brownstone hit the ground running with the sock in his mouth. He ran with his body kind of sideways, back steeply arched like some sort of tiny, much cuter than normal and oddly athletic rodent sized camel. Adorable.

Timmy shrieked like an aged hyena who just had it's purse stolen, then ran after Mr. Brownstone. Bobby sighed like the extremely tired man he was and ran after them both. The King stayed in his coma. The portal closed.

27

Nothing happens in Chapter 27.

    …I lost Chapter 27. Hopefully, nothing happens in Chapter 27. Fuck.

28

You keep pushing. You know what needs to be done but you can't move forward. Fruitless-internal-emotional-struggle, oh ye virgin mother of inaction. I keep pushing, but emotions outpace thoughts, and thoughts outpace hands.

This is what you are here to do. I hear you. This is who you should be. I hear you. This is how you are supposed to feel. I hear you. Now fuck off.

My apologies. I woke up this morning to a giant timer here in my lovely little room. Bob's putting pressure on me now. The sand is slipping away towards oblivion and I don't even know what any of this means. Honestly, how much time does a six-foot tall sand clock hold anyway? If all the ticking mechanical clocks weren't enough, now I get to listen to the end of our universe approach with the sifting of sand? I think Bob wants me to lose my mind. I'm sure there's a lesson to be learned. Some intricate plot twist in the mystery novel of existence that insists upon my lunacy for the moral of the story to be revealed.

Since you have no way of knowing as you read this, I will just tell you I've not been writing for quite some time. Nothing that came out felt correct, so I stopped. Instead of writing I've been doing a lot of calisthenics. Lots of calisthenics.

And now this. As if writer's block isn't bad enough, here comes Bob with a giant hour glass full of sand. I hear you Bob, but this was your idea you know? I didn't specifically ask to be ripped away from my family and transported to a interdimensional office full of fucking clocks and told I have to write a book about anything to save the universe, did I? Did I?

Well shit. Maybe I did. Not in so many words, but maybe I did. And now here's this damned hour glass. But of course, it's not really an hour glass. It's a, "you have no idea how much time this represents, so if you thought you were going nuts before, well fuck you," glass.

In exactly the right amount of words…I deserve this.

A Prayer:
"Dear Bob, when all is said and done, please, forgive no one. Amen."

It can't be Hell if we're all there together, can it?

Section 3

29

Daffodil opened her eyes as slowly as she could, uncertain if she wanted to know where she was. Then they were open. Blink. There was Tom standing in front of her. She was in her bedroom. No, this was nicer than her real bedroom. This was the version of her bedroom that she fantasized about, the one she gave herself in her head when she closed her eyes and laid awake at night. "Where am I?"

"You're safe," Tom said.

"Oh." Suddenly, for the first time, Daffodil wondered if she should be afraid of Tom. She went on and closed her eyes again. It's easier to pretend shit ain't real with your eyes closed.

"Tom?"

"Yes?"

"You were my imaginary friend."

"I was never imaginary."

"Oh, I always thought you were." Daffodil sat up in the bed, eyes still closed. She decided to be as quiet as possible for a while. Best thing to do was just be quiet and let her mind get going at its own speed.

Tom would have sat but he was a ghost so he didn't bother. Standing didn't hurt his knees anymore. Besides, he wasn't sure she wanted him anywhere near her. Tom was no genius but he had come to know the girl pretty well, watching her all these years. She was frightened and she had every right. Things were only going to be more difficult from here on out.

"Okay Tom, where am I? And please don't say someplace safe." Before Tom could answer Daffodil continued. "I mean, of course I want to know I'm safe, but I want you to tell me where I really am. Don't dance around."

"I think maybe it would be best if you…did you really think I was make believe all this time?"

"I still think you're make believe. I'm either dead, or in a coma, or I have finally lost my mind. None of this feels real. I don't feel real Tom." Her eyes were still closed.

"What do you want, Daffodil?" he asked her softly. All she did was make a slow, mumbled sound of tiredness. "I'm sorry little one. I'm sorry. I just don't know what to say to you darlin'. I think maybe you should just rest. There'll be plenty of time to talk later."

"*Am* I safe here Tom?"

"I thought I wasn't supposed to say that again."

"I changed my mind."

"Yes. You're safe."

"Thank you." She held her hand in the air for Tom to take, and he did. He'd learned a few things over the years about being a ghost. He could touch now. Daffodil pulled him down and he sat next to her, placing his arm around her. To her surprise, and comfort, she could feel warmth in his embrace. She fell back asleep.

Tom didn't know what to tell Daffodil, or better stated, didn't know how to tell her what he knew she would need to understand. It wasn't the words to use. There were only so many ways to describe the situation. His problem was when to fess up. How would he know she was ready to accept the truth? Should he be sensitive? Or simply be pragmatic? Was his hesitation to explain really about his own uncomfortable emotions?

Daffodil sat in her bed. She was eating chicken soup. "I know this isn't real, Tom," she said.

"It's real enough. I'm real. You are too. The rest of this stuff is just window dressing."

"Then what does it look like in here when I'm awake?"

"You're awake right now," he said. He was a little confused. "If you think you're dreaming, where do you expect to be when you wake up?"

Her face changed expressions.

"Never mind. You're awake. I promise." He paused for a moment until he was convinced she believed him. "It's not as nice when you're asleep." Tom twirled his finger, indicating the room.

"You mean dangerous?"

"No, I mean not as nice," he said. "It's more boring when you aren't awake. Just an empty old room." He chuckled a little.

"Why?"

"Well, that's just the way it works. You're in charge."

"Tom, stop making me ask questions. Just explain everything to me."

"I'm sorry. Let me ask you a question."

Daffodil sighed, but relented. "Okay."

"Do you like your soup?" He smiled his most charming smile.

"Yes."

"Good. Please just eat. Get your strength back. I promise, I will explain everything when you're better rested."

Daffodil smiled and continued to eat. She stopped asking questions for the time being. This might seem hard to believe given the situation, but as with the rest of her body and mind, her curiosity wasn't yet running at maximum power. Besides, the truth might make the nice room and the chicken soup go away. She realized she wasn't necessarily ready for whatever might come next. Tom wasn't going to hurt her, and it was just the two of them. So, she was going to finish her food and then maybe go back to sleep for a while. That seemed like a good plan.

Daffodil woke up and screamed. The room was pitch black. There was no Tom.

"Tom!"

There was no Tom. She got out of the bed and began to rustle about the room blindly, feeling her way. Everything she touched seemed like commonplace things you might feel in a bedroom in the dark, but at the same time unfamiliar. There was no mental image in her head for anything she put her hands on. She was about to freak out, lost in what should have been a small room, and now she was afraid she wouldn't be able to find her way back to the bed to hide under the covers. Just before she panicked, Daffodil realized she could hear something.

She followed the sound across the room and discovered a door. She placed her ear against the surface. There was a commotion on the other side. There were doors slamming and screeches, and all sorts of other noises. Whatever was happening on the other side of the door sounded like pure hysteria.

The door handle jiggled. Daffodil yelped and grabbed the knob, trying to keep it from twisting. She couldn't stop the handle from turning, but the door didn't open. The handle continuously rotated and something outside slammed on the door powerfully.

"Stop it! Stop it! Tom! Help me!"

Whatever was trying to get into the room stopped and the handle sat still again. Daffodil sank down to the floor and curled her knees up into her arms. She stayed silent and listened for a while, trying to figure out what was going on out there. She thought maybe she would just close her eyes for a while and sit very still. This had worked for her before.

Daffodil opened her eyes. She was back in the bed again. The room was lit and cheery. There stood Tom with more of that damned chicken soup. "Where did you go?"

"Oh, just to run some errands."

"What's going on outside? I could hear things. They sounded like monsters. There was no light in here. I found a door, and someone, something, tried to get in."

"Don't worry," he said. "I told you, you're safe in here. The door is locked and no one can get in but me. I have the key. See?" He held the key up for her inspection. Not so comforting as he might have hoped.

"So what's going on out there?"

"Well it's real busy outside. There's just a lot of folks out there looking around you know. Moving from here to there."

Daffodil used a new face on Tom. He knew exactly what the expression meant. Her patience was up.

"It's a hallway Daffodil. People are using it to get from one place to the other. That's all. Just a bunch of hallways filled up with doors to other places."

"I heard commotion Tom. I heard people, or something, out there screeching and making all sorts of scary noises."

"Well, nobody is supposed to be out there at all. Unfortunately, some of those who are don't get along. We're in a special place, but it's even more special because of you."

"Tom, that's very sweet but I am not going to the prom with you."

"What?"

"It's very nice, and you can flirt all you want, but I am not going to the prom with you if you're gonna treat me like a child."

Tom blushed. *She made a joke. That's good!*

"Tell me where the hell I am Tom. I'm tired of chicken soup. I want to know what the fuck's going on, and where I am, and what the hell I am doing here and all of that shit." The look on her face was stone cold. I've seen it. That face either means I'm in serious trouble or we're about to have red hot relations. I rarely know which until after.

Tom didn't know Daffodil cursed. He did not like her use of foul language. I do.

Tom didn't want to tell Daffodil she was mentally being pulled to pieces. He didn't want to tell her that she was split up into a thousand personalities in her head, and that they were all trying to take over. He did not want to explain to her that an alternate dimension had accidentally been dumped into her subconscious, and that it had caused her brain and the alternate dimension to malfunction, to somehow merge. He didn't want to tell her that this odd predicament her brain was in had also made her extremely vulnerable to nonsense like ghosts and demons messing around in her mind.

He told her.

She took it pretty well, all things considering. Let's be honest though, her entire life had pretty much sucked. The things her parents did were more than terrible. Tom's news may have been bad, but at least she wasn't getting raped and beaten.

"So, this is my brain? You and me, we're in my brain? So right now, I'm just a thought?"

"Yes."

"Then why can I touch and feel?"

"You have a very powerful mind."

"Oh fuck you Tom."

They both laughed with maniacal exuberance, crafted in the fires of fear and isolation.

Just in case I haven't explained this well, I will reiterate. Inside Daffodil's mind is an alternate dimension, a singularity that functions as an interdimensional gateway to every place in our universe. This singularity used to be hidden on Curtis Gout's butt as a birthmark shaped like a shoe. The gateway dimension isn't normally open to the public. But, because it was accidentally hotwired into Daffodil's brain, it malfunctioned and all hell has broken loose.

Some ghost or spirit invaded her when she was a child and then exited through a door. When that ghost or spirit left, something on the other side of that door came inside. And so on, and so on, until the next thing you know doors are flying and creatures are coming and going and no one is wiping their shoes. Meanwhile, maybe because her parents did lots of drugs, or maybe because the alternate dimension got stuck in her head, or maybe because Bob simply wanted things that way, Daffodil's mind was fragmented into multiple personalities. There were hundreds of them, if not thousands, and they were all battling for control of the body. Now that I think of it, it may have been one of Daffodil's splits that initially wandered into the gateway dimension and opened the first door. There's really no way to tell.

What I do know is this. The Daffodil that I love, the one that you know, she's the most important. She's the real deal, the alpha, but when she went through the portal she jumped right into her own mind. That is simultaneously the safest and most dangerous place she can be.

"What are we gonna do, Tom?"

"I don't know. I'm sorry, but I wasn't really given much coaching on this. You're safe here for now. A lot safer than you were on the outside, so that's good."

"What about my body? If I'm in my own head, where's my body?"

"Well," Tom made a hesitation face. You know what the hesitation face looks like, when someone is trying to soften a blow or just doesn't want to say something. "Right now it's in the future."

"What do you mean my body is in the future?" She almost screamed.

"Well, the thing is, one of your 'Others' is in charge right now, and when you jumped through the portal that brought you here, it took your body to someplace in the future. You aren't running the show anymore."

"What the fuck Tom!? How am I supposed to feel about that, huh?" Now she was screaming. "God knows what I'm doing out there and there's nothing I can do about it! Besides the fact that this is all really fucking screwy to begin with. I'm in my own head for Christ's sake! What good are you? Why are you even here? I might as well be sitting here by myself with no answers to any of this shit than, than, well than knowing half of what is going on and not knowing what to do or how any of it really works! How can I be inside my own head Tom? Huh? How can someone be in their own fucking head!?" She began to cry. She mumbled apologies to Tom and he held her and rocked her back in forth. The idea of her body being out there wandering around without her had really disturbed Daffodil. In a lot of ways, her physical being was all she had, and it wasn't hers anymore. This was going to take a lot more sleep.

When Daffodil was asleep, Tom was doing everything he could to protect her. He had lied. There were creatures that were going to come through that door if he did not maintain his vigilance. There was one in particular who we've already met that was looking for her right as I typed these words. Tom was also keeping an eye on her body. He had one of the special watches. Curtis had given it to him. The watch could lead him to Daffodil's body and open portals to bring him back into the hallways. He could shove Daffodil's body through the portal if he had to, but he could not control where it went. This was a problem.

Another problem was her body bouncing around alternate dimensions and alternate timelines all on its own, without the need for a portal. When our Daffodil jumped into the portal and wound up inside her own mind, we're pretty sure the anomaly was caused by the portal's existential transference happening simultaneously with the hostile take over of Daffodil's body by one of her others. Whether our theory is correct or not, her body was shooting randomly from one place to the next throughout all existence. There was no pattern. Some places she rested for minutes, others for what seemed like years. She moved forwards and backwards through time, and all the while the different versions of her would take turns at the wheel, driving her body through life. This made it very difficult for Tom to track her. He was constantly fighting his way through the hallways of her mind, following the watch, looking for the right door to take to find her body. And Daffodil was a magnet for bad news. Every time one of her splits took control of her body they wound up getting her into trouble, but there Tom would be to save the day. Poof! Into the portal she goes, where she winds up, nobody knows.

Daffodil and I were destined for one another. Had to be. There's no such thing as coincidental romance.

While Daffodil's body was bouncing around the universe, winding up in all sorts of trouble, Bob had seen fit to move me around on Earth. Forwards and backwards through time and on a few different planes of existence, but always on Earth – except for a brief stint in Hell.

I saw Daffodil for the first time in the future, but we didn't speak. Later, I saw her inside this crazy barn with a bunch of Hip-Hop farmers. The group was sort of like the anti-Ku Klux Klan, and they were having a secret rap hoedown. But, for me the circumstances were ill-fated. There was something following me at the time. I'm not sure if it was the devil, or one of his minions, or someone helping Timmy, but either way I was scared shitless. There was no opportunity for me to engage her. I took note though: Pretty girl keeps appearing in my adventures. Seen in future and at present day barn dance. Keep an eye out for this one.

Then there was New York, a special occasion. I was still sixteen at the time. That's when we finally met. Obviously I know now that Daffodil has more personalities than the sun has reasons to shine, but I met *her*. I met the real one. She was herself in New York.

Daffodil woke up again, still in her imaginary bedroom. Tom was gone. There were dim lights on and she lay staring at her ceiling. Was there a rocking chair creaking forward and back? Was there a woman humming? Daffodil leaned forward and there sat an older woman, perhaps in her fifties, working on a ball of yarn. There was a trail of knitting behind her. Daffodil didn't bother to try and determine what the lady was creating.

"Gosh, I miss being so pretty," the older woman said.

"Who are you?" Daffodil was not taken by the complement. She was absolutely frightened. That might not be quite right. She was full of the tension that can quickly become many emotions, often fear. That instant surge of uncomfortable energy, and we have no idea what emotion it will translate to. Where it will take us. That's what Daffodil felt.

"Who are *we* dear?" the woman said matter-of-factly. "That is the question, because I am you." She said the last three words slowly and distinctly.

"How did you get in here?" asked Daffodil.

"Don't worry about that. I'm not really here."

"Oh, well that makes perfect sense. Okay then, what are you doing not really here? How are you me? Why is it that no one will just explain their self without playing all these games with me?"

"No one is playing games. Tom was trying to let us figure things out on our own, when we were ready. It's really hard to know how much to try and teach someone and how much to let them discover on their own. He was just nudging us in the right directions. I'm here because you brought me. Tom told us most of what was going on and why, but he left out a few things. We have a purpose we need to discuss. Time is beginning to speed up. We will have to take action soon."

"Stop calling us we. It's irritating."

"Sorry. Force of habit."

"This is a habit for us?"

"No, I just say 'force of habit' a lot as an excuse. We say that a lot. Someday you may start saying that a lot. What is the best way for me to refer to us without irritating you?"

"Never mind. Now you remind me of me."

"We get that saying from Truant, you know."

"Who's Truant?"

"Well shit. Sorry. Don't worry about that yet. The point is that you have some more running to do. You can't stay here forever. Bob has a plan for us."

"Who is Bob?"

"Damn it. You don't know that yet either. I have got to watch my tongue. Look, here's the deal, girlie. I am obviously an older more knowledgeable version of you. I am here because I was sitting at home knitting and I fell asleep and when I woke up I was here. You brought me here. This sort of thing has happened to me before, and will happen again to you, so you will get used to it."

"What the fuck?"

"Daffodil, learn to save that word for special occasions. It's more effective." She spoke with a motherly tone. "This is never going to end. You'll have the ability to roam around in your head from now until death, but we're going to calm things down in here." The older version of Daffodil was striking when she chose to let herself glow emotionally. The younger version of Daffodil realized she was staring at the woman she could someday become and it thrilled her. For a moment she was that woman. Confident, and knowing, secure in her words and her presence. "Listen. He's out there, and he is coming for you."

"How can you be here telling me this?" asked Daffodil. "When you were my age, did an older version of you come back and tell you these things?"

"It doesn't work that way."

"How does it work?"

"This is your mind Daffodil. You tell me. You're in charge here. I know Tom has said the same thing to you and this is something you really need to wrap your head around." She said that last bit with a wry grin and a little hesitation on the word "head." "Life doesn't make sense Daffodil. You can only spend so much time trying to figure life out. The rest of the time you have got to keep moving."

"Well then what is the point to all of this?"

"You tell me."

"Tom lied. There is something out there trying to get me. I can feel it. I can feel all of them out there. I just don't want to."

"You have to."

"I know. Tom said my head was the gateway to everywhere. I have to get to somewhere. Somewhere else in my head, outside that door. I have to get back in charge. How do I do that? And how did I know about Truant? Is that the name you said?"

"Yes."

"How do I know about him?"

"Just think about it Daffodil. I'm not going to say anything you don't tell me to."

"I've already seen him. I already know him."

"We're bouncing around through time and space right now darling. Your others can't do anything that you can't see if you really try. They're all separate, yet all connected, and you are the centerpiece."

"You really aren't here, are you?"

"Well, not physically, no. But I have a body. I'm not just a manifestation. I exist elsewhere."

"I'm seeing my future?"

"A little bit. I may be your future, I may not."

"Okay. If I leave here, how will I know where to go?"

"You just will. There is a pull. You can feel it if you try. If you concentrate."

"What about Tom?"

"Tom is going to die."

"How do we know?"

"You can feel that too."

"I don't want Tom to die."

"It's too late."

"No!"

Daffodil shot up in bed. She was dreaming. It was a dream. Now she was awake again, really awake. The room was pitch black and there was no Tom. Daffodil turned on the lights.

30

urtis Gout stared at the wonderful old lady's face. He'd finally recognized who she was. He chuckled mildly – in his brain – ever so often as the thought bounced around in his head. This made perfect sense. Such a pleasant thing, to spend some time with someone you love.

He felt confident she knew what was happening. She at least suspected. Her puzzling efforts had become more restless. The old lady searched more intently for every piece now, never setting them aside in haste. Each piece was well acquainted with her soft crooked fingers. She turned them in her hand, studying them from all sides and remembering each point of view so that she would recall the piece faster if she saw a possible fit. After memorizing its features, each unused piece was set in a very specific place on her table so it would be readily attainable when she thought she'd found the correct spot in the puzzle for it. Then she forgot.

Unfortunately, the goofy old broad had some issues with forgetfulness, and those issues led to regular use of the phrase, "Now where did I put that damn piece?"

Dementia. What a pisser. This she also knew. She understood she was suffering from memory loss, though sometimes it would take her awhile to remember.

Either way, Curtis felt sad and relieved and nervous all at once, from one passing moment to the next. There was nothing he could do to help. Apparently, she couldn't hear his thoughts, and to make matters worse, the stories that were once oozing from her mind for Curtis to absorb had gone silent. He'd hoped there might be some clue to his escape in her psychic transmissions, but she was too focused now to project any of that stuff. All that came out was a simple rhyme from time to time.

"Look who's knocking on the door. The monster's coming back for more. Run, run, run, there's no escape. Pieces for puzzles, it's not too late. Pieces for puzzles, it's not too late."

31

Pieces for puzzles, it was not too late, as Mr. Brownstone ran down an alley behind a block full of buildings on the bad side of a town whose name I don't know, on a planet whose name I cannot pronounce – or spell with the keys available, for that matter. In a stroke of bad juju, Timmy wound up on the same planet and was now perilously close to our friendly ferret.

Mr. Brownstone scurried under dumpsters, a breath ahead of the monster, who smashed each dumpster aside with a roar as he grew closer to his prey. Mr. Brownstone made it to the end of the alley and found himself trapped. There was a door to the left and a door to the right. He shifted into his humanoid form and opened the door to his right, revealing a portal. *Praise Bob.*

Timmy reached for the back of Jerry's neck. Just as Timmy clasped his hand, Jerry Brownstone dropped to the floor, a ferret once again, and jumped through the portal. Timmy followed Mr. Brownstone back into Daffodil's mind.

At the same time as Timmy and Mr. Brownstone arrived, Bobby Gout stepped out of another door at the end of the same hallway.

Here was the scene: Bobby was at one end of the hallway, Mr. Brownstone had made his way to the other, and Timmy stood in the middle just outside the door he and Mr. Brownstone had both used.

The monster alternated his gaze between Bobby and the ferret. Timmy didn't know which one he wanted to kill more. Bobby did not hesitate. He charged Timmy, screaming his head off, and the monster waited.

Currently, Timmy was a seven foot tall mud creature. There were sticks protruding from his muddy body in various places and he seemed to be swarmed by an assortment of bugs, buzzing about him fervently. Serpentine creatures that looked like snakes were oozing in and out of his flesh.

Bobby's hope was to buy Mr. Brownstone time. He charged the monster with all his might, only to be smacked against the wall with little effort from Timmy. Bobby sank to the floor, nearly unconscious. Luckily Mr. Brownstone had no plans for escape. Yes, this meant Bobby got whacked about for no reason, but at least his failure didn't hurt the team.

There was only one door our friendly ferret Jerry Brownstone was looking for now. The time for a stand had arrived. Mr. Brownstone scurried in between other creatures' feets and paws and dangly thingies in search of a sign. A few creatures tried to stomp Mr. Brownstone for no particular reason, other than simply having nasty personalities. Most of the creatures in the hallway cowered, due to the presence of Timmy, who destroyed as many of them as he could along his way. A few lives were saved merely because Timmy was losing sight of the ferret and didn't want to waste time killing.

Daffodil and Tom were sitting on mats in a gymnasium training facility, about to get back to work on their situation. This was her new version of reality, the same space she'd previously fashioned as her bedroom. Daffodil no longer found comfort in the coziness of her bed so she had turned the room into a gym. There were free weights, a heavy bag, a speed bag, a sparring ring, even a basketball hoop for Tom. After all, Tom was the one helping her learn to control her environment.

Daffodil had made the decision to retake control of her body, really the only choice she had if she wanted to survive. Daffodil and Tom knew she could control her other selves to a certain extent. At least briefly, they could be manipulated. So, Daffodil had been meditating on using her other personalities to help her find the control room of her brain. "Tom, even if some help me, I'm going to have to fight other versions of myself, aren't I?"

"I hope not. We might be able to sneak you where you need to go."

"I don't think that will work," she said flatly.

"Why's that?"

"It's a feeling I have. This isn't going to be easy. I have this feeling that it's not supposed to be, and that we're going to win anyway."

"Well, I suppose that's a good thing to know, or feel. At least you won't be let down if you're wrong and things go smoothly."

"Oh I don't know," she said with a smile. "I think I might be a little."

"Be careful what you wish for, darlin'," said Tom, smiling as well but in a forewarning manner.

"Just a little bit I said!" She was charming as could be. "What am I supposed to do when I get to where I'm going?"

"I don't know. I really don't. I wish we had help, but all I knew was to protect you, and hell, that was years ago when he told me to do that. When Curtis came to me he just told me about how special you were, and to keep an eye on you until he came back. Then he shows up one day and says, 'okay, it's about to happen,' and he tells me I will take you through the portal soon. That I will know when the right time is and that he'd come find us when another time is right, and then he disappeared and he hasn't come back. Honestly all this 'time is right stuff' gets on my nerves. Thomas Jones is a man of action."

"Tom, did you just refer to yourself in the first person on purpose?"

"Yeah, I was curious how it would feel. What did you think?"

"I think if you're going to do it you should use your full name."

"Thomas Jones is my full name," he said. "I ain't got no middle name."

"Are you sure?" she asked with a grin.

"Thomas Bankshot Jones is a man of action!" Tom said it with a ton of false bravado. "How'd that work for you?"

"If you weren't so old and dead I might have a crush on you now."

"You sure about that?"

"No," she said with deadpanned honesty.

"Yeah, didn't work for me either." They both laughed wholeheartedly.

Mr. Brownstone took a left and two rights around corners at the ends of hallways. All was the same in the maze. The doors all looked the same. The hallways all looked the same. A whole bunch of the female humans looked the same. All of them actually. They all looked exactly alike except for that one little thing. Whatever part of an individual's personality that shows through on them physically, that little piece of us that makes sure we really have no true twins in life, those little pieces were different.

Jerry had no idea where he was going. All he knew was he had to keep running. The door would be there. He knew it. That is just the way things worked. Of course he had no idea where "there" was, but he knew "there" is where he would eventually wind up. Mr. Brownstone believed in fates like that. After all, he was alive wasn't he? The last of his kind. That will usually fill a creature with a heightened sense of purpose.

It would be there. The damn door would be there. He would find the correct one and he would know it was the correct one when he did. That is how things would be. That's right, dammit. Keep telling yourself that Jerry.

Jerry Brownstone was beginning to lose hope.

Timmy was staring at a creature made of light whose movements created music. The melodies were soft and soothing. Timmy forgot about his pursuit of Mr. Brownstone for a moment. The creature's name was Sharuth. It was an Intilescent. The Intilescents were a soft-spoken race. They liked leisure activities and rarely left the comfort of their own hometowns, let alone their own planet. They had the technology for space travel but preferred spending their intellects and resources on a healthy and peaceful planet. Sharuth had wound up in the gateway dimension accidentally. Poor thing.

The dark void of Timmy's hand held Sharuth by the light of what would have been its neck, if it were human. Sharuth tried to wriggle free which just made more music, and of course, intrigued Timmy further. The Intilescents were beautiful creatures. Sharuth was terrified. The music of his movement was still lovely, yet not enough to soothe a beast. Timmy remembered the key and the sock and the ferret and he devoured Sharuth where he stood. Another soul was lost. Timmy marched on.

Bobby woke in the hallway still slumped against the wall. Creatures were still shuffling past, but as his vision cleared he realized he was surrounded by sets of legs that weren't moving. He looked up and understood that he was staring at the girl. They were all her, and it scared the shit out of him. They looked angry. No, more than angry. They looked sinister. He tried a welcoming grin. One of the Daffodils to his left stepped forward and kicked him in the face.

Daffodil was trying to focus on her others, trying to see what they were up to, but it was like shuffling through thousands of images all at once. The images flew through her mind's eye so quickly it was almost impossible to decipher anything. Tom watched her face squint with determination. The images slowed as she gained control. "Tom, something's wrong."

"What do you mean?"

"Holy shit, Tom. We're beating a black man to death!"

"What? Who?"

"I don't know who Tom, and I sure don't know what this guy is doing in my head!"

"Well apparently he's getting his ass kicked, that's what he's doing."

"Not helpful, Tom!"

"Do you think its Curtis?"

"How would I know if it was Curtis? I don't know what he looks like!"

"Well, he's black."

"Tom!"

"I'm just sayin..."

"Just saying what, Tom?"

"It would just be really helpful if it was Curtis, that's all."

"Well not if he gets beat to death!" screamed Daffodil.

"Well you're the one doin' it!" he screamed back at her. To which she replied with a simple, crystal-clear frown. Tom's face apologized for the rest of him. They were both under a lot of stress.

"Alright, I'll go out there and try to stop you."

"No, Tom. I've got to do it. Besides, it's not just him. There are others."

"What do you mean?"

"There's something running from something else...like a rat running from a monster. Maybe. I don't know what they are but I think I'm supposed to help the one who's running away."

"Well that makes perfect sense."

Mr. Brownstone was exhausted. He felt like he'd been running for hours upon days upon weeks. He had, and it was no way for an expectant parent to finish carrying its child to term. He looked over his shoulder. The monster was still behind him, nipping at his heals.

Ever so often, he could see Timmy pause long enough to study some other, never before seen creature. The encounters always ended the same. The other creature ceased to exist and the monster would be back on Mr. Brownstone's trail.

Timmy had taken the form of a demonic robot. Instead of legs, his torso rested on treads like a tank. He had snapping claws for hands and the head of a robot clown that spun in circles constantly. A tail of colored streamers billowed from an exhaust pipe. "Flight of the Valkyries" blared from speakers in his chest. Timmy had a flare for theatrics.

Bobby was trying to defend himself from the Daffodils. He didn't want to hit a girl and he certainly didn't want to hurt Daffodil, and he was afraid if he hurt one of them he would hurt them all. So basically, he was getting his ass handed to him by a bunch of teenage girls who all looked and sounded exactly the same. The assault was painful, and fucking creepy.

Mr. Brownstone began to notice arrows lighting up on the ground beneath him. Uncertain the arrows were meant for him, the message was made clear when he came to the end of a hallway. He looked right, no arrow. He looked left and an arrow appeared before him. He went left. Someone was guiding him.

Timmy caught a giant chicken man and burned him alive in a deep fryer that extended from the rear of the truck part of his robot body – kind of like a really really hot tub in the back of a limo. Timmy then changed his head from a robot clown head into a flesh and blood clown head. Let me just say that the neck area where the flesh of his head met the metal of his robot body was a nasty mess. Disgusting.

Anyway, Timmy ate fried giant chicken man for the first time in his life, and it was delicious ya'll.

Bobby saw one of the Daffodils punch another one of the Daffodils in the face. Then another. Then another. The next thing he knew he was watching an all chick brouhaha. If he weren't in an extreme amount of pain, if the girls didn't all look exactly the same, if they weren't sixteen years old, completely insane, and actually pummeling one another, the scene may have been enjoyable.

Hell, who am I kiddin'? It's still pretty damn hot, he thought to himself sarcastically.

"Am I turning you on?"

Bobby looked up. One of what appeared to be the good Daffodils was staring right at him. She had her hands wrapped around the throat of what appeared to be a bad Daffodil. He blushed.

All at once, every Daffodil paused just long enough to look at Bobby and say, "Gross, dude," then went back to beating the piss out of one another. Bobby opened his mouth to defend his decency. He would never…

"Would you just get off your ass and get moving?" the nearest good-guy Daffodil asked. "This isn't fun for me."

"Seriously, I would never," Bobby pleaded.

"Just go!"

"They're coming, Tom."

"Who?"

"All of them."

"Should I unlock the door?"

"Not yet."

"What do you think we should do?"

"I don't know. I was hoping you might have an idea."

"Um…uh-oh?"

32

Mr. Brownstone took a left into a long empty hallway with a single door at the very end. Hysteria clamored behind him. He scurried down the hall, as only a ridiculously cute ferret could.

Timmy turned a corner and charged into a throng of startled, confused, and angry creatures. They were excited and on the charge like stampeding cattle. Timmy ran amongst them, lost in the glut of the hunt. His excitement for terror and destruction was pulsating from him as he rapidly changed forms from one horrible representation of evil to another.

Timmy made it to an intersection. To his left he saw Mr. Brownstone scurrying down the empty hallway. He screeched triumphantly as he chased after the ferret.

"Tom, open the door." Daffodil spoke with the firm urgency of sudden recognition.

"Okay."

"Quick!"

"I'm on it." Tom hurried across the room and threw the door open to the oncoming madness. He stood with his mouth agape as Mr. Brownstone ran between his legs and into the room. Mr. Brownstone quickly changed into his humanoid form. He was naked. Daffodil did not have time to blush.

"Shut the door!" shouted Mr. Brownstone.

Tom was already in motion, but too late. He slammed the door shut onto Timmy's hand. Timmy roared in agony, shoving his face through the crack in the doorway, snapping at Tom with the head of a dragon. Daffodil screamed. Mr. Brownstone rushed to Tom's aide.

"Who are you?" Tom asked.

"Jerry Brownstone. Security Minister to the King of Shar-Crypt-On, last child of the planet Kilotilla. I'm here to help." Mr. Brownstone spoke with a grunt as he and Tom attempted to stand their ground. "I have the key. She has to tell me where to take it."

Timmy pounded on the door.

"Daffodil, are you listening?" Tom strained against the door. A ghost that has learned to touch has much greater strength than when they were human.

"Of course I'm listening!"

"What do you think?"

"I don't know! What key? We need time to talk about this."

"I'm sorry miss," said Jerry. "But I don't think we have much of that."

"Well who ever said anything about a damn key?" Daffodil made her way to the door and added her weight to the barrier.

"Don't mean to be rude," said Tom, "but are you pregnant?"

"Very," said Jerry. There was no opportunity for a dramatic reaction to Mr. Brownstone's impending parenthood, as a powerful blow from Timmy hammered the door.

"Daffodil," said Tom. "Darlin', we gotta do something."

"I know, Tom. I know, but I don't know what to do! You never said anything about a key or a naked animal man."

Tom smiled at the girl. He truly loved her like a daughter. He put his hand on Mr. Brownstone's. Jerry looked at him and knew what Tom was about to do. Mr. Brownstone stepped back from the door, pulling Daffodil with him, positioning Daffodil around behind him, holding her away.

"No!" she screamed. "What are you doing?"

"I love you little girl," said Tom. It was the first time in her life anyone besides her brother said that to her.

The door swung open violently. Timmy stood still, just outside the entrance, with an expression the mixture of surprise and blood-lust. "Here I am, big guy," said Tom, then he stepped through the entrance and pulled the door closed behind him.

"Tom, no! Don't! Tom!" Daffodil began to cry as she screamed.

Mr. Brownstone rushed across the room and locked the door. He turned back to Daffodil. "I found you. I can't believe I found you! I've been looking everywhere, but I had no idea…who or what. That's what made searching so hard. I had no idea what I would find."

There was a thud against the door. A scream. Tom's scream. Daffodil screamed with him, then said, "We have to do something!"

"I know," said Jerry. "I know. We've got to get this key somewhere safe."

"But, Tom!"

"Tom is not the key to our existence. This is." He held up the sock with the key in it.

In her dismay, and shock, and confusion, she screams, "That's the key to existence?"

He takes the key out of the sock. "The gateway to all points of existence was somehow placed inside your brain, is part of your brain. There's a door hidden in here somewhere this key fits. I think we're supposed to go through that door and lock the key inside so no one else will ever be able to get in."

"C'mon you big ugly turd! I'm right over here!" Tom was shouting outside.

"Tom?" she asked meekly.

"Here," said Mr. Brownstone. "Take this. Only you will no which door it belongs to. That's the only way I can make sense of any of this."

"Why me?"

"Because it's your head."

Daffodil took the key and held it with her eyes closed. There was another loud thud from the hallway. She flinched, eyes pinched tight. Time paused. Daffodil froze the room around her, the entire supernatural world that was her own mind. She travelled inward, to a memory, and returned with a glimpse of her past tightly gripped in her hand. She released it into the air, bringing the images of the memory alive in the room. Mr. Brownstone watched as the room swirled into a blur around them, a mixture of the vision of her dream and the gym he'd just been standing in.

"I had a dream about this once," she said, her voice taking on a calm, trancelike quality. "A long time ago. I was very little, maybe five or six. It was a really bad dream. I woke up in the middle of the night and all I could remember was the door and the key and people being hurt and being really scared. But all I could see was the door and the key. It was a nightmare."

"Then that's the answer," said Mr. Brownstone. "That's where I must go." He gently took the key from her hand and returned it to the sock.

"Where?"

"Into your nightmares."

Tom was slowly but surely being beaten to...well, he was already dead. Perhaps beaten to expiration is the best analogy. Early in the fight, Timmy had difficulty figuring out a way to hurt Tom. His punches and kicks and fire breath and all the other things he tried to throw at Tom simply passed right through him. Eventually the monster understood and his attacks began to suck the life right out of Tom's very soul. The attack on his soul was agonizingly painful. To Tom, it felt like having every fiber of his being pulled apart one molecule of energy at a time. Like peeling a bandage off of his soul's nervous system as slowly as possible, only a billion times more excruciating.

"Tom's already dead, Daffodil," said Mr. Brownstone, as the young woman flinched at the sound of another terrified scream. "He'll be okay. When we open that door you're going to get him and take him with you." Less than five minutes had passed since Tom had gone outside to face the monster, but that time had been filled with torturous screaming from her friend, which made five minutes feel much, much longer than five minutes.

A plan was in place. Daffodil was going to take her body back and Mr. Brownstone was going to enter her nightmares. Hopefully, once she was back in full control she would be able to see the door and guide Mr. Brownstone. He would find the door to Euphoratopadopia – although neither of them knew that is where the door led, or what Euphoratopadopia was for that matter – and take the key in with him, locking the door behind him for forever. Then, in that unknown place, he would have his baby. Surely he would be safe there. Right?

The only problem with the plan was what to do about Timmy, but Daffodil thought she had an answer. "They're almost here," she said.

Tom's appearance was now one of a ghost-man who had indeed been in a fight for his afterlife. He was bleeding unreal amounts of unreal blood. His face was battered, black-eyed and swollen lipped. They were reflections of how he felt emotionally. That's all he really was anymore anyways, really. He was a conscious energy, and currently the only thing he was truly conscious of was pain. Timmy was about to devour him. Tom looked away, turning his head from imminent destruction. Just as his blurred vision gave way to the infinite darkness, Tom thought he saw something.

"Hey, fucker!" Bobby Gout turned the corner into the hallway and saw Timmy holding what looked like a human being up to his monstrous face. Behind Bobby marched a fleet of Daffodils. Every one of them was now dressed in combat clothing. Some were Ninjas, others Army Rangers, and more than a few wore comic book super-hero-esque costumes.

"Hey fucker!" they shouted in unison.

Timmy tossed Bankshot Jones the ghost aside, turned toward the Daffodils, and licked his lips.

"Are you ready?" asked Mr. Brownstone.

"There's someone with them. It's a guy we were beating earlier. He's with them."

"Bobby?"

"Who's Bobby?"

"A hero. A great warrior. It must be him! He's here to help. We stick to the plan. Once you get out that door, no matter what happens, you've got to stick to the plan."

"I will."

And with that, Mr. Brownstone threw the door open.

33

It's me again, Bob. Bob? Are you there? No? This is for you then. Not for Bob but for whomever you are. I know you won't say it, but you can feel it too, right? You can't say it because you're too frightened. Or maybe you won't say it because you're too respectful. But I can, because this is the truth and she knows. Fuck you, Bob. There, I said it.

She knows, she knows, she knows, and she most likely doesn't even exist. Don't lie to yourself. Don't pretend that half of life is reality and the other half is open for interpretation. Choose not to believe if you will, but somewhere in your heart of hearts, it's not a lack of belief, but merely a lack of acceptance. Lack of proof. Call it science or nature or God or Bob or nothing at all, but the chaos is real. That's what Bob really is. Chaos. That's how life sprung forth. Chaos. Pre-existence of life, nothingness, was an era of supreme organization. Supreme order. Bob is chaos, and those who purport to recognize this chaos, to live in the really real world, even those enlightened few are the victims of their own delusions, myself included. We wrap ourselves in the security blankets of our own perceptions, just like the rest of you. Where's my woobie?

I have been, and always will be, a glass half full kind of guy. I swear. But right now the glass is half full of piss. I am confounded by impermanence, baffled by the trappings of sentience, and eagerly awaiting the ridiculousness of my next five minutes because I have no idea how this story ends.

Even here in this room as I write testimony of the universe's secret absurdities, I cling to the notion that life is meaningless in effort to numb the pain. But I don't want life to be meaningless, I just don't want the pain. There's got to be a way to change the rules of this game. A way to get out alive. I've chosen love to save me. Hers.

I'm not the only one. Many choose love. Others choose hate, money, food, children, trucks, drugs, fucks. The list goes on and on. Keep heads down and place one foot after the other. Drown out all the noise and find some daily satisfaction with yourself and your surroundings. Bless you, go and be happy. You probably earned it in some former life, or by luck of the draw, but don't kid yourself into believing happiness had anything to do with you. We are reactionary vessels, acting with genetically predetermined and environmentally programmed solutions to a never ending onslaught of stimuli in the midst of an infinite organism. Hmmm, my woobie is super cozy.

So, when people ask me how I know Bob is real, besides the fact that I have met her, I tell them Bob is real because she has to be, otherwise my entire premise for existence is a fraud. Besides, who else stuck me in this stupid ass room? Who else makes you do all the bullshit you don't want to? Clean your room, floss your teeth, save this fucked up universe…

Everybody's got a Bob. That's what we're dealing with. This is what's going on in your under-brain when everything should be okay but nothing is. This is why we desperately seek peace, or a buzz, or violence. This is why lives are lived in constant states of avoidance until the face is slapped with mortality and the biological clock ticks its witching hour, when the walking dead start begging and bargaining their way to eternity. Meanwhile, the reproductive have begun the programming of their seeds, the next generation of Bob's victims, hoping with aggressive futility to pave their offspring's way into a charmed life.

So many of us are scared to say, "Fuck it," while those that aren't afraid are rubbing our noses in lives that we're too frightened to achieve. The bastards take what they want and apologize later, and despite my current predicament in the universe I can't promise you they'll someday get what they deserve. Meanwhile, others have actually accomplished what we wish we could without cutting corners. They've treated people nicely, held their heads and moral standards high, and expressed their humility before Bob, or nature, or their loved ones, or whatever the stupid shit is that they believe in, and they make us feel worse about ourselves than the fuckers that don't deserve awesome lives. Whether it's Bob, or simple nature, or a man with an animal head you have to ask, why not me? Why can't I have that life? Why Bob why? To get me the right truck? That joke makes no sense here!

I'm not trying to hurt anyone or scare anyone. I sure as hell realize there are tons of people out there who are as well aware of this whole reckless situation as I am and have somehow managed to find solace. They have managed peace and that is beautiful, and reverent. Hopefully you will as well. Hopefully, in your life you will spend more days smiling than frowning. Hopefully, you will love and be loved, trust in whatever it is you choose to believe in and more often than not, find yourself satisfied. I swear this is earnest. I want those things for other people despite my contempt, because I know with whom my contempt truly lies. My contempt is not for humanity, or with Bob, or with no Bob existing at all, or with the possibility that this one pass through the maze is all we get, all that we really are. Here is my problem: I hate myself, maybe a little bit more than I should.

Anyway, while I was bitching and moaning, throughout existence a whole bunch of babies just died. Happens all the time. I suppose I should get back to work. Fuckin' Bob.

34

Everything went wrong. Immediately. The plan wasn't that great to begin with, though the conditions under which it was formed were admittedly unreasonable. In their hurry, Daffodil and Mr. Brownstone had not accounted for certain things which, to be fair, they had no way of accounting.

For instance, it just so happened that Timmy was much closer to the door than Daffodil and Mr. Brownstone had hoped. Close enough to knock them both to the floor with one large smack. His hand morphed into five giant snakes instead of fingers. Daffodil and Mr. Brownstone were pinned to the ground by the snakes. Rows upon rows of hooked teeth snapped at their faces while Timmy's eyes remained focused on the army of combat Daffodils.

Bobby led the girls into battle. They charged Timmy, letting out war cries at the top of the lungs. The monster stood his ground with his captives behind him.

Tom slowly rose on shaky legs. "Daffodil, I need a big knife."

"What?"

"Give me a big knife or a sword or an ax or something," he said.

"Just use your head."

"Oh," she said. "Okay," She briefly pinched her eyes closed and there it was. Tom swung the knife and chopped off Timmy's snake hand. Timmy roared. Daffodil turned her head to Mr. Brownstone. "Go."

Timmy saw Mr. Brownstone begin to run off and threw a trap at him. The snare caught Mr. Brownstone's leg and Timmy began to reel him in. Bobby Gout tried to step in to free Mr. Brownstone but got flogged on the head in the foray. He staggered back from the battle as a battalion of Daffodils reengaged the monster. Timmy killed them at will.

On a side note, as the other Daffodils die our Daffodil gets stronger and gains more control over her mind. Surprise!

"Daffodil," said Tom. "You gotta go, darlin.'" A spear plunged through Tom's chest. It was attached to the previously severed arm of Timmy, now re-grown.

"Tom!"

Timmy turned on our Daffodil. A third arm protruded from his torso and the new hand squeezed her throat. Bobby made his way to Mr. Brownstone. He cut the shapeshifter loose from the snare and Mr. Brownstone limped off down the hallway. Timmy felt the tension ease from the trap-line and realized his prey was getting away. He roared as he tossed Daffodil aside, transformed himself into a raging bull, and barreled down the hall after the rodent.

Daffodil held Tom's head in her lap. Bobby Gout stood behind her. The feeling he had was familiar. Compassion and concern watered down by their opposing duality, the emotional emptiness, of knowing. This ghost was his friend, though they'd never met. This ghost was dying.

"Tom." That's all she could muster. She was crying again. Every time Daffodil thought she was completely wrung out of sorrow and tears they both returned.

"It's okay," he whispered. "I'm a ghost, remember? He can't hurt me."

"I need you to stay."

"I'm not going anywhere."

"You're..." (sniffles) "...fading."

"Oh that," said Tom. "It happens. Don't worry, darlin'. You're gonna be just fine." Then he was gone. The final blow from Timmy had pinned the tail that was Tom's soul to the overgrown ass of eternal mortality. The next phase of Tom's existence was set, the blessing of everlasting rest.

All that remained was the portal-watch Curtis Gout had given Tom for him to track Daffodil with. Daffodil picked the watch up, cupped it in her hands, then pressed it against her chest as she wept. Bobby crouched next to Daffodil and tentatively placed a consoling hand on her shoulder. "I know it hurts but we need to move."

"I know."

"You get where you're going. Okay? Try not to think too much. Just keep moving. He's not really gone. I promise." Bobby was lying. He had no idea.

"I'm fine." She grew cold to the touch and Bobby pulled his hand away.

"I've got to go help Jerry," he said.

"Who?"

"The ferret."

"Oh, right."

Bobby stood and pulled her to her feet. "I've got to go. Don't worry, Daffodil. Someone will always be with you."

"How do you know?"

"That's just how this works," he said. Then he did something simple and unexpected. He took her hands in his and held them until they both felt the warmth return to her presence. When he pulled his hands away, she had placed Tom's watch in his palm.

"You might need this."

Bobby gave a solemn nod of his head then turned and took off after Mr. Brownstone.

Daffodil stood where Bobby Gout left her. Her eyes were closed as she centered her mind. Her focus was on control. She was feeling around for it, searching, listening. Before long, revelation found her. One of her "others" that was with her, there in the hallway, had been to the control room. Daffodil felt the pull. The tug of life called her forward.

Funny thing about focus, as one thing becomes clear another may grow cloudy. While Daffodil had gathered her thoughts and focused on where the control room was located, she had relinquished her hold on the other versions of herself. There were still dozens of Daffodils alive in the hallway, but they were no longer hers.

A short glance revealed to Daffodil the change in their faces. They had each regained their individual will. Fear blasted adrenaline through Daffodil's veins. She was already in trouble again.

"I guess I just can't catch a fucking break, huh?"

All of the others smiled at her. A smile with a single word meaning. A single word, the answer to Daffodil's question, with no need to be uttered aloud or heard: Nope.

35

Darius was sitting on a large, sturdy limb not far up his tree. Of course, the tree didn't actually belong to Darius, but he'd been with it for so long a sense of ownership had certainly grown within him. After all, Darius had counted and learned the name of every leaf and branch on Kyle.

Our secret weapon rested in a perfect state of thoughtlessness, a quiet space in between any passing dialogue in his mind, when he saw the new leaf appear. First, a tiny bud sprouted. Then the bud quickly uncurled itself into a full-grown beautiful leaf. Darius smiled at the wonder of creation. *Hi Tom!* he thought. *So wonderful to see you again!*

36

Mr. Brownstone, Timmy, and Bobby Gout were back to their "race for the ages." Mr. Brownstone reached the entrance to a dark hallway that none of the other creatures in Daffodil's head would enter. Strange that nothing was coming out of the hallway, but that is the key to nightmares, is it not? Repression.

Mr. Brownstone entered cautiously. This place was reminiscent of a damp alley deep in the bowels of a sordid red light district, shortly after the witching hours of debauchery and shame. The hallway was lined with doors, just like all the others, but nothing was coming or going from any of them. These doorways were to Daffodil's hauntings and meant for no one else but her.

This didn't make sense. Mr. Brownstone understood why the other creatures in Daffodil's mind wouldn't enter this hallway or attempt to use these doors. What he didn't understand was how nothing was entering from behind those doors. Why weren't the nightmares trying to escape? Oh well, he shook the thought off and moved forward.

Despite knowing time was of the essence, he still moved slowly. He was a full grown, proud creature, but he was frightened. There was a monster chasing him that destroyed entire planets and could consume souls, and Mr. Brownstone was genuinely more terrified of this girl's mind. Jerry might be asexual, but he had known plenty of gender based species, and he knew damn well the scary shit that went on in the dark places of their minds. A sexual creature's fear is nothing to be trifled with.

Shortly after Mr. Brownstone entered, Timmy discovered the pathway into Daffodil's nightmares as well. He stood at the entrance and smelled the air, as if it would mean something to him, but he was only delaying the inevitable. The childish intellect of the monster was intimidated by this place. The voice in his head was already chastising him, but the rest of him ignored the nasty voice. He did not want to go in. Everything in there was bad. He could tell. This place was full of nastiness.

But you are bad.

What? He shakes his head.

You are bad. You're the scourge of the universe. You do bad things. You devour souls. You are perfect evil. A god. You destroy. You're the destroyer. You create fear. You are fear, and you're going to bring this selfish, happy go lucky universe to its knees.

Oh. Okay.

Well?

Well what?

Go get the damn rat, idiot!

But...

But what? Do we really think anything in there can hurt us?

No, of course not.

Then what's the hold up?

I think, nothing in there will be frightened of us.

Who cares? You can still destroy them. Besides, nothing in there is real.

But I like it when they're afraid. They taste better.

Are you sure you really want to destroy the universe?

Yes! Of course. Why wouldn't I want to destroy the universe?

Well, you're sort of dragging you're feet here. Is it because we'll be all alone again? There won't be anything else around to be afraid of you. Nothing else to destroy.

No! This universe will be destroyed. I hate it. I will consume every life-force in its body, crap their souls, and watch them all float through the cosmos for eternity as worthless space poop!

So you're going to celebrate your triumph watching space poop for eternity?

Shut up! We're going to get the key.

Okay, okay. All that really happened was Timmy paused for a second at the entrance to the hallway, sniffed at the air like it would mean something to him, then walked on in after Mr. Brownstone. We must remember this cretin rarely behaved with any reasonable amount of self-awareness. Any and all of the previous and following dialogues between himself and his self are purely speculative, because fetishizing him as a moron made him easier to deal with emotionally. At least, it did for me.

Bobby Gout turned the corner just as Timmy walked into Daffodil's fear factory. *This is it,* he thought. There had never been an option of turning back. The thing is, sometimes it's easier to participate in something when there's no end in sight. It's a different story though, when conclusion looms in the not-distant-enough future.

Bobby had no idea how this could end. There was no fighting the monster, not with any of the limited means available to him. Jerry was pregnant for goodness sake. How in the hell were they going to prevent the thing from winning? For that matter, why in the hell had they just led the monster closer to where it wanted to go in the first place? Basically offering up the key to existence on a freaking platter? Whose idea was that? Why Bob why?

Don't say it, Bob.

Don't do it.

To get you the right truck, Bobby.

Arg.

37

Curtis felt the ache of long suffered pain refresh in the old lady. He felt it in his own bones, in the ebb and flow of the universe. The torment was a memory for her. For Curtis, brand new sensation. A very present crashing of melancholy tidal waves.

The monster was winning and the old lady was exhausted. Curtis could feel the desperation radiating from her and infecting him as well. Encouragement was attempted with projected thoughts of hope and strength, but he suspected very little could influence her now. The old lady knew she was dying, and she wanted to. She was ready, weary and looking forward to a long, well deserved rest. The way things are meant to be. The only problem was she knew it wasn't yet her time...time, time, time...

There was still work to be done, even as she slipped away. This conflicted state of being left her frantic. As frantic as she could possibly be in her aged, energy depleted body. The old lady wanted to want to finish the puzzle, but she didn't, but she knew she had to, but she was desperately ready for the oncoming quiet. The internal conflict was unfortunately laughable, if she'd had the energy to laugh.

Keep going little lady. You've got to keep going.

Another piece of the puzzle is pressed to the table, fingers delicately massaging and kneading the cardboard cutout into position. Curtis doesn't know if the piece is in the correct place, if it fits. *Oh well,* he thinks. *Bob's will be done.*

38

Daffodil's Others were hot on her trail as she raced for the control center of her mind. As much as she wanted to, standing her ground was not an option, despite her suddenly increased strength. While Timmy had unwittingly made Daffodil more powerful by killing a considerable number of her alter egos, she was still severely outnumbered.

As she ran Daffodil wondered how the ferret and the stranger were doing. *What were their names again? Bobby and Mr. Brownstone?* Everything had happened so fast, but she had a feeling she would meet them again someday. Maybe. Hopefully.

Daffodil made it to the control room. There were a few minor scrapes along the way with other versions of her self. For the most part, when they crossed paths, she busted them up with a quickness. Daffodil had decided that inside her own mind she was the bad ass, the alpha bitch. If she later determined she no longer enjoyed the "COME GET SOME" tattoo she'd imagined across her shoulder blades, when this was all over she would make it go away.

When our Daffodil entered the control room she quickly dispatched of the Daffodil who was operating her body. This wasn't pretty, folks. She strangled herself to death with her own bare hands.

In the control room was a massive switchboard with dozens of monitors hovering above. The motherboard operated a surveillance station that accessed everything happening in her mind. Besides "video" relay from all the hallways, there were birds eye views from all her Others as well. Daffodil could toggle between all the different versions of herself and see everything they saw.

There was Mr. Brownstone, running through the picture on one monitor and into the picture of another. The ferret-man looked lost, or confused. Daffodil scanned her nightmares for signs of the correct door, even though she had no idea how she would know which door was correct until she saw the obvious choice. Deep inside her nightmares, at the end of a long corridor, was the only door with a keyhole. She sent Mr. Brownstone a tour guide.

Once the path was set for Mr. Brownstone, Daffodil noticed something else in the control room. A switch, curiously labeled "Switch." Guess what the switch was for? Daffodil guessed, and then she flipped the large white lever. All of the sudden she could feel her body again, but she was apparently having a seizure. Daffodil would eventually learn that seizures occurred every time her body swapped personalities.

On this occasion, being new to the process, Daffodil wondered if she should stick a wallet in her mouth, then told herself no, as she remembered it's impossible to swallow your own tongue, at least while it's properly attached. When the seizure finally ended Daffodil passed out from the sheer emotion of the event. When she woke, she realized she was resting in a dumpster.

I found Daffodil in a dumpster. I believe I said earlier that I worked for a time in a restaurant in New York City? Maybe not. Either way, I did, and one night when I made the end-of-shift garbage dump, there she was, covered in filth and looking for food. Or so I thought.

She was dirty head to toe and stunk to high heaven, and I still fell head over heals for her. I had not yet had a real girlfriend at that point in life. Not sure why but that feels relevant.

Our initial greeting was odd. I said her name was beautiful and she made fun of my parents for their choice in mine. I'm fairly certain she liked my bird more than she liked me. (Back then I had a bird named Mr. Cool who traveled everywhere with me, even to work. Mr. Cool spoke to me once. Legitimately spoke to me, not some cheap grifter parrot's copycatting parlor tricks. More importantly, Mr. Cool saved my life once. He's moved on. I miss him very much.)

Daffodil had this crappy orange Yamaha dirt bike parked in the alley (she found the keys in her pocket…). At the time she lied and said her parents had given it to her. Apparently, at some point one of her Others had stolen the bike. Anyway, I offered her some food in exchange for a ride and she begrudgingly accepted the barter. I fed her and off we went, cruising the streets of New York City until the early morn. Much later, after I learned of her dissociative condition, I finally understood why she'd had so much trouble driving that motorcycle. To be clear, my Daffodil had never driven a motorcycle.

We fell in love almost instantly (at least I did), and spent the next two seasons falling further into that love. This was the greatest era of my life. Everything since then has been a less enthusiastic by-product of that wonderful, fanciful, romantical age of newly born and purely formed love.

Okay, okay, that's not true. Just waxing romantic hyperbole. The truth is life got even better, but it got worse first.

One minute our pregnant ferret Mr. Jerry Brownstone was completely lost in Daffodil's nightmares, immersed in the replay of a beating given to her by her foster father, the next he was chasing a wind-up mouse sent by Daffodil. Of course, since he was in her nightmares, it was a super-scary-nightmare-wind-up mouse.

As Mr. Brownstone approached the door he shifted into his humanoid form and took the key from the sock. Just as he moved to put the key in the lock, he felt a giant hand wrap around his head. Timmy squeezed Mr. Brownstone's skull near the point of implosion, but before Mr. Brownstone's head caved in Timmy rotated the naked man to face him. The monster took the key from Mr. Brownstone's hand and held it in the air, gazing at it with childlike wonder as he continued to squeeze Mr. Brownstone's head. A bloodthirsty smile beamed on Timmy's now apelike face.

Bobby found Jerry and Timmy just in time. "Stop!" he shouted. Timmy turned towards Bobby and stared, mildly confused but mostly annoyed. Bobby sort of shrugged his shoulders and lifted his hands slightly, a sheepish grin on his face, as if to say, "I meant, stop please," or, "Please don't hurt me," or both at the same time. His mind raced. There was no fighting Timmy, but Jerry was in trouble. What to do, what to do?

The monster's apish appearance triggered an idea, and Bobby, to his own surprise, started to hambone. Completely out of character for our very serious hero, Bobby was jiving and slapping his legs, bouncing back and forth from one foot to the other. Silliness to soothe the savage beast. Apparently, Timmy enjoyed the show, as he began to grunt like an amused gorilla and changed the shape of his head accordingly.

The next thing he knew, Bobby was babbooning his way around the hallway, doing his best impersonation of an orangutan – I'm going to plug as many simians here as possible – with one arm over his head and one arm dangling as if dragging the ground. Timmy let go of Mr. Brownstone, who fell to the floor, then got into the act with Bobby. The monster shrieked like a chimpanzee and danced an Irish gibbon's jig. If the universe hadn't been hanging in the balance, the dance-off would have almost been fun.

Bobby worked his way closer to Mr. Brownstone, but in a very nonchalant manner. So nonchalant in fact, he grabbed Timmy for a quick, two-macaque tango. A little colobus cha, cha, cha. Surprisingly, Timmy let Bobby lead.

When he was close enough to Mr. Brownstone, Bobby made his move. With a quick one-two-two-one dance step, he shoved Timmy away to full arm's length, then reeled the monster back in, then sent the monster spinning down the hallway.

Bobby dropped his act and dove for Mr. Brownstone. All he needed to do was shove Jerry through one of the other doors before Timmy realized what was happening. Wherever the door led was safer than here, he hoped. Bobby threw open the closest door, dragged Jerry in front, and rolled-shoved Jerry in.

Timmy's rotations ended with a masterfully timed matador's pose, the monkey business having come to an end with the dancing fool's spin. When Timmy saw what Bobby was doing he spit the long stem rose out of his mouth in disgust. Now he was mad. The monster morphed back into a bull and charged down the hall.

Bobby got Mr. Brownstone all the way through the door and slammed it shut with just enough time to wish Jerry well before Timmy reached him. Timmy barreled into Bobby, knocking him into the wall, then morphed back into a humanoid form and bonked Bobby magnificently hard on the head. Bobby crumpled to the floor once again. Winding up knocked out on the floor was becoming an unfortunate habit for Bobby Gout.

Timmy stood before *the* door with the key in his hand. There were no markings. No glyphs. Only the keyhole and handle.

This was a big moment for Timmy. Why wasn't he already walking through the door? Was he paralyzed by the magnitude of the moment, or was the big jerk savoring his almost-achievement a little prematurely? I wish I could say he had no reason to gloat.

He stood and stared and stood and stared. Then this whole scene gets downright irritating to deal with, and I think to myself, "You motherfucker you," as I'm typing this out, because Timmy changes shapes again and this time he looks exactly like Mahatma Gandhi. A giant, muscle-bound, extremely well fed Mahatma Gandhi, and that really bothers me (perhaps more than it should have, considering the circumstances) 'cause Gandhi was a cool freaking dude. I don't know if Timmy knew what he was doing or if it was just a sick accident. What I do know is he put the key in the lock to the door to Euphoratopadopia – the most pure place in all of existence, then he unlocked the door, threw it open, and right before he walked in said one word with a smile on his face.

"Peace."

39

There was something very important I was acutely unaware of during my initial courtship of Daffodil Fields. Okay, okay, there were quite a few things, but my lack of skill at physically pleasuring the female species has no place in this narrative. (Daff, that one's for you, baby.)

I was a kid for Bob's sake!

Whatever. Let's just stick to the nuts-and-bolts, the aspects of universal intrigue I was unaware of, and call it a day. For starters, although I had already been told I was going to save the universe, I had no idea Daffodil and I were going to do so together. I was still young and dumb enough to be working under the assumption that I was somehow more important than other people. This was an easy mistake to make when you've been granted access to the blueprints of the universe, the wonders and mysteries of the Bob.

The funny thing is, everyone has opportunities to save the universe. I've simply had more than average and been royally slapped in the face by mine. Most people have at least five opportunities to save the universe in their lifetime. They just happen and you never know when. Bob needs a smile. A wife looks at her husband and smiles just then. Universe saved. Bob needs a shoulder to cry on. Someone who believes in him is talking to him and actually takes the time to ask Bob how his day went. Universe saved.

Seriously, this shit just happens. No rhyme. No reason. Perhaps (insert your name here) recently thought fondly of an old friend, and that friend's ears burned, and they thought back fondly about you (whoever you are), and that warm exchange of thoughts was exactly what Bob needed with his cup of tea this afternoon. Boom, universe saved.

Another thing I was frightfully unaware of was where Daffodil ran off to when she was away. She came and went as she pleased, of course. That is one of the benefits of being homeless. People don't often know where to find you. So, I was constantly waiting, hoping, praying that she would return. Now I can tell you exactly where she was going. For the most part, back inside her mind.

Unfortunately for Daffodil, despite her efforts in self-defense, many of her Others would find ways into the control room. Whether they picked the locks, kicked the door in, crawled through a brain duct or dumb-lucked their way through a portal to the room, Daffodil was in constant battle with her Others to maintain control of her body. The internal conflict was harrowing, and violent, but she always won, and every time she grew even stronger.

Back to our courtship, from my perspective. One day she left and didn't return. The last time we saw each other had held a few awkward moments. Myself, being quite the novice in the ways of love in those days, and remaining so as I type these words, feared for the worst. She was gone. I had said something wrong. I must have.

The failure was agonizing. Life was over. I was such an idiot. So stupid. How could I have done whatever it was I must have done? At some point I had obviously let my guard down and behaved like the person I actually am? Crap! How could I have let her catch me off guard? Ruined. The whole thing just ruined. Man was my heart broken. Now I know her disappearance had absolutely nothing to do with me.

Darius was lying with his back to Kyle, enjoying the purple and green hues of an Euphoratopadopian sunset. There were animals around lazing in the grass or stopping by for Darius to give them a pat before they headed home for the evening. Far in the distance was a set of treeless rolling hills lush with tall grass. Suddenly, a figure began to rise over the crest of one of the hills. Darius squinted to discern the shape, the shape of a man.

Darius was neither frightened nor happy nor excited in any other manner. He was curious. The animals who'd been socializing around him gathered close. They wanted to know what was going on. Darius let them know he thought maybe they had better take off somewhere and hide. Most of them stayed.

Bobby Gout woke with an aggressive headache. The battered hero laid still for a while, wondering what to do next. Strange how our mind's work sometimes but the fact Timmy left the door open didn't register with Bobby until the door began to shut. To be fair, he'd taken a pretty good jolt to the brain vault.

I suppose a gust of wind happened along that decided the door was in its way. Who knows? One way or another the door began to swing shut. When Bobby realized the door was closing, which meant it was currently open, he rolled into action. Bobby rolled and flopped and landed one of his legs next to the door jam so the door could not close.

A deep, rumbling groan began a long, slow trip from the depth of Bobby's lungs. The sound accompanied the activation of his body as he slowly rose to his feet. Finally up and at 'em, Bobby stepped through the doorway. The first deep breath of the freshest air he'd ever breathed in his life not only refilled his lungs, it removed the pain from his head so quickly he couldn't remember how badly he'd been hurting. This was the most gorgeous place he'd ever seen. Bobby smiled and began to run.

After the last time Daffodil and I had seen each other in New York, the meeting I mentioned earlier that was followed by her disappearance, the specific disappearance that sent me on an emotional snipe hunt through the forests of self-loathing, after that meeting I would eventually learn that Daffodil had been pulled back into her head again. Another one of her Others had penetrated the control room and assaulted her.

She dispatched of this one rather quickly, then napped for a while in the control room while her body slept on a park bench in Washington Square Park. At this point Daffodil knew there was nothing that could happen to her body that most likely had not already, barring major dismemberment. – At one point she had apparently lost the end of the third toe on her right foot, which had quite honestly been one of her favorites. All of her toes curl slightly differently from one another at their ends and that one had been amongst the cutest of the bunch.

Anyway, it was during this nap when she heard Darius' voice. "Daffodil, come." was all he said.

When she woke, she knew where Darius was. Suddenly, she knew the monster and Darius were in the same place. Daffodil left the control room and her body to the whims of her Others and ran back into the hallways of her mind. She would not need a key. The door would open for her. This was her head dammit, and in her head, Daffodil was king. Not queen. King!

Darius stood with his back to the tree. Timmy stood facing Darius. They were one-hundred yards apart. Darius didn't need any notice as to what Timmy represented. This was what he'd been built for. Darius felt the truth in every fiber of his being, as much as he'd learned to feel the breath of the planet he'd been living with for so many years. Darius was a man in his prime now, full blown into adulthood. The perfect mixture of lessons learned – even in virtual solitude the lessons were there – and physical prowess.

The monster took a step towards Darius, who held his hand up telling Timmy to stop. Timmy did not. Instead he took another step forward. Darius opened his mouth to say the word, "stop," but no words came out. Darius had not spoken in the many years he'd lived with Kyle the Tree and all the animals. When he opened his mouth to speak a green energy shot forth with incredible force, sending Timmy flailing, flying, and landing many miles away.

In very short time, Timmy returned and roared at Darius. Darius opened his mouth in defense once again, this time roaring back with a sonic boom and pure, bright red energy. Timmy struggled forward against the light as the animals began to attack Timmy in support of Darius. While the energy continued to blast from his mouth, tears streamed down Darius' cheeks as he watched many of his friends die.

Bobby heard the sonic boom far in the distance and knew that was where he should be heading. He was running the wrong way. Bobby corrected his direction and hustled forward day and night, somehow trading the years of his life for ludicrous speed. He would age ten years on his last quest to find Timmy, but he would arrive for the conflict in phenomenal physical condition.

Daffodil stood in front of the door. The nightmares hadn't bothered her as she passed. Having already lived most of them, they didn't really matter anymore and certainly couldn't hurt her anymore. Not after what she'd been through.

With a firm hand she turned the knob. The trap freely slid clear of the doorjamb, the door swung open, and Daffodil walked out into a pasture filled with the flowers for which she was named. She could see two small, person shaped figures off in the distance with some sort of energy or light flashing between them. Daffodil took off running as fast as she could.

Bobby and Daffodil had almost made their way to the fight, but Timmy was almost within reach of Darius. Darius stood with his fists clenched at his side, letting loose every ounce of energy that had been storing inside him since he'd found his splendid home. The warrior collapsed to his knees and still the light blazed.

Darius saw his sister off in the distance as the light blasting forth from his mouth began to wain, then his powerful assault came to an end. All of his energy was spent, his job was done, and he smiled as he fell backwards to the ground.

The gentle, loving soul in Darius' body did not have an opportunity to escape. Timmy stood over Darius, extracting the soul from his physical vessel. Even though Darius was successfully defeated the monster still wanted to eat him, if for no other reason than spite.

Daffodil was the first to reach Timmy. Without hesitation, she leapt onto the monster's muscle-bound-Gandhi back. Timmy swatted at her but his overgrown muscles had rendered him inflexible. Herky-jerky attempts to swat Daffodil threw Timmy off balance, causing him to stagger about whilst flailing his arms like an oversized villainous toddler taking its first evil steps.

Not knowing what else to do, Daffodil held on as tight as she could and bit down on the back of Timmy's neck with all her might. The monster howled with pain. Encouraged by Timmy's cry, Daffodil continued to rip at him with her teeth. Dark smoke gusted from his wounds, fueling the fires of his rage as our rabid hero spit out a chunk of monster flesh and let whoop a war cry meant for Timmy, her foster parents, and every other hateful, hurtful motherfucker who'd ever lived. With vengeful exuberance she went in for another bite.

Daffodil kept biting and biting and biting and biting (Feel free to skip ahead to the last "and biting". There are twenty-six of them in this paragraph. Go ahead, count them, or just read on.) and biting and biting and biting and biting and biting and biting and biting and biting and biting (Why twenty-six?) and biting and biting and biting and biting and biting and biting and biting and biting and biting and biting (Because that's how many times she bit him.) and biting and biting and biting.

Despite the ferocity of her attack, Timmy was finally able to throw Daffodil from his back. Then he picked her up by her hair, turned his arm into a stone-handed jackhammer, and bludgeoned her face with rapid-fire punches.

Bobby gained an incredible amount of speed in the closing distance between he and Timmy and was charging at a super human pace. As Daffodil's eyes rolled back in her head, Timmy drew his massive hand to strike her again. Before Timmy could drop the hammer Bobby rammed the monster at full speed. The blow sent Timmy flying once again, this time with a handful of Daffodil's hair ripped free in his grasp. Daffodil laid crumpled on the ground several feet away. Bobby dashed over and tried to rustle her awake.

Timmy rose and began the long walk back to his prey. Again.

Daffodil's eyes regained their focus. With no more than a grunt for a thank-you, she crawled free of Bobby's grasp and worked her way towards Darius. When Daffodil made it to her brother, she found his lifeless eyes wide-open and a smile upon his face. With a kiss to his forehead she said hello again and goodbye all at once.

Suddenly, Timmy's shadow loomed large. Bobby quickly opened a portal with Tom's watch and grabbed Daffodil. There were encouraging, desperate, urgent words muttered uselessly by Bobby in attempt to nurture her towards the portal. In the end, he simply over powered her and sent her away. Daffodil couldn't see the new leaf bloom on Kyle, who welcomed Darius home forever. The portal closed. Daffodil, though a young woman, was the last child Bobby would save, and perhaps the most important.

Sure as fuck was to me.

And then there were only two, the monster and the hero. The end was near, and Bobby did the only thing that came to mind, he stood still. Indecision would not matter. How in the hell was he supposed to fight this thing anyway?

The dark smoke seeped from Timmy's wounds, reaching for and enveloping Bobby Gout. Timmy held his arms forward and wielded the smoke like a weapon, pushing more and more in Bobby's direction. Bobby was maddened by emptiness and rage and fear. Any attempt to resist the all-encompassing gloom was futile, especially when the emotions Bobby was assaulted with so closely resembled the emotions that had powered him all these many years while chasing the monster through the cosmos. Was this the honorable death for which he'd prayed? Failing at his mission, consumed by his own darkest thoughts and emotions?

Bobby closed his eyes and said hello to Bob. Our man on a mission begged reprieve, and then he was gone. Without a blip he disappeared within the maelstrom of darkness by which he'd been surrounded. For a moment Timmy was confused. Then he was triumphant! The monster cried victory aloud, and with very poor sportsmanship, pointed at Kyle as if he'd just scored sportsball points against the tree's defense. I suppose, in a sense, he had.

Timmy walked over to the tree, circled it, ran his left hand along its trunk, and whispered sweet nothings to his newest victim. Hands forward and clasped together, Timmy watched as they changed shape. The handle of an axe extended forth as his appendages merged, and from the handle grew the blade. And with that ax Timmy began to chop down existence.

The monster whistled while he worked. The tune came from Sharuth, the Intilescent he'd killed in Daffodil's mind. For Sharuth, it had been a death song.

40

I remember a dream from the last time I slept. I was staring at Kyle and I was crying. Bob stood right next to me smiling at her tree, but the dread I felt was insurmountable, as if she weren't present.

"Why are you crying?" she asked.

"Because I don't know," I said.

"Don't know what?" she asked. "I'm right here."

I saw her lips move but I couldn't hear. Bob put her arm around me for comfort but I could not feel. I wept on, uncontrollably. Time passed. I aged.

Then, as years blinked passed and I grew old, I remembered she was with me, her arm still around me. I turned to gaze upon her but instead I fell away from her embrace and landed on my knees. I raised my head and she said, "I'm right in front of you. Would you please smile?"

"But I still don't know."

"But I'm right here," she said. I don't think she was frustrated.

"No," I said, shaking my head.

"What do you mean, no?"

"I'm sorry. I don't mean it that way. I… I'm always lost."

"Child, you're exactly where you are."

"But I don't know what's real. I don't know if this is real."

"But I'm right here."

"I just don't know," I replied. I spoke sternly so she knew where I was coming from.

Bob ushered me back to my feet then punched me in the stomach. "Now, how do you feel?"

I doubled over in pain and coughed exhaustion. "Is this all in my head? Is this all in my head or are we really doing this?" I asked, in between coughs.

Bob smiled and shook her head with what looked like mild exasperation. Then she laughed at me, gently, and tapped her wrist. "Time's almost up," she said.

Sometime later, I woke. Who knows what happened in between there.

41

Timmy was chopping down the Tree of Souls. Curtis Gout was locked in a jigsaw puzzle. Bankshot Jones was at peace. Darius was at peace. Bobby Gout was dead, or something. Mr. Brownstone was Bob knows where.

I knew none of this, way back when…

The next time I found Daffodil she was hiding behind the dumpster at work. Well, I say I found her. Now I know Bob sent her to me. Bob and Bobby Gout that is. Badly bruised and shaking, I took her home – home being a small room in the basement of the restaurant. I cleaned her up, nursed her back to health, and our romance continued. Looking back, knowing what I know now, how she let go and fell in love? To be frank, she ran emotional circles around me. It's like she just turned off all the stuff that happened to her and erased the pain, at least for a while.

When she is being sweet, Daffodil says she was able to ignore everything that had just happened to her because she was so smitten with me. When she is being playful, she says it was because she was in shock, and that's the only way I got her panties off to begin with. When she is being mean, she blames me for the whole damn thing. Even though I wasn't there! It stops being *our* destiny and becomes *my* destiny, and it's my fault she is stuck dealing with all of this bullshit. Man, I miss her right now.

What happened next for she and I was sort of typical, I suppose. Right. We were together for months, loving, and nursing her wounds. One day, we were on one of the many bridges in Central Park. We both say, "I love you," for the first time, at the same time. Normally this moment probably would have been really cute. Daffodil and I both immediately ran away.

I was running because I was overwhelmed with fear because I loved her and I was caught up in all this supernatural shit. There were agents of evil with flaming eyes all over the city watching me. I was afraid she would get hurt or something. I don't know, it just happened. I have to admit when I realized she had also ran away I was pretty confused. To be honest I still am. She's never really admitted what that moment meant to her, or why she fled. I leave her alone on stuff like that.

Here's the thing. While Timmy was trying to chop down Kyle, the Tree of Souls, I was moping around trying to figure out what I did wrong, feeling sorry for myself, all the while trying to decipher the prophecy from a visionary young child named Frank. I met Frank in the future before I met Daffodil. Frank was the first one to tell me I was going to save the universe.

Anyway, I finally came to the realization that Daffodil was the whole point of my quest to begin with. Everything I had been through was about her. I'm in love with this girl and I've got to find her. The universe depends on it!

"Chop, chop, chop," said Timmy.

Here's another thing, the universe's continued existence really did depend on me finding Daffodil, but not because of our love for one another. Still, I went searching for her out of love. Perhaps infatuation at first, but in the end, love.

My search took awhile. When I finally found her she was about to commit mass suicide with a bunch of free spirits led by a group called the Men of Foot. Daffodil had traveled with them since leaving me. She doesn't really say much about that time in her life. I honestly think she just sort of shut down emotionally and wandered with these people. Hundreds had fallen in with them, and the Men didn't ask many questions. They clothed you and fed you and otherwise left you alone. Not a bad group really, except for the mass suicide thing.

Anyway, they were all jumping from a high ridge in the Grand Canyon – none of them died by the way…another story, another day. I saved Daffodil's life. I drove my motorcycle off the cliff, jumped off, and caught her. Then a friend of ours saved us both. He's this guy we know who has wings. I mentioned him before, really early in the book. The one that would eventually preside over mine and Daffodil's nuptials. The goofy bastard can fly and do some other cool stuff, and he's very happy to share how fantastic he is with you. In spite of himself, mí amigo is a lovable braggart. We're still not sure if his species are angels or not. Bob won't say. Either way, while Daffodil and I were falling to our deaths I blew a special whistle and there he was, showing off with his wings, swooping in to save us both from crashing to the Earth. Show off.

By the by, in case you're wondering, I've intentionally omitted his name. Trust me, the playful slight will stick in his ribs and much friendly laughter will come at his expense for many years. All's fair in love and teasing your loved ones.

Back to point, there's only one reason I'm telling you this, why this is important. Okay, I immediately admit that's not true. Life just isn't that simple, but for the scope of my assignment there's only one reason why any of this is important. That's not really true either. Damn that is anti-climactic.

How about we just go with: There's an old lady about to finish a jigsaw puzzle. There we go.

The old lady is Daffodil Fields, my love. Someday, perhaps when I have more time, or when I damn well please, I might tell you more about my search for Daffodil. About my personal quest to save the universe for the first time. About Daffodil's life in between year sixteen and old age. About our friend with wings and all sorts of other things. For now though, none of that matters. For now, in this story, all that matters is her life was saved. Daffodil had to live, she had to grow old, and she had to finish the puzzle.

Curtis Gout stared up at Daffodil from his prison. She held the final piece of the puzzle in her hand. The key to his cell. The old lady smiled and Curtis felt relief flowing from her. Then he felt something else. Memory. Daffodil's life was flashing before her mind's eyes, and in these unusual circumstances, Curtis' as well. This would be her end. Curtis felt so sad to see her go yet so pleased for her all at once. His friend placed the final piece of the puzzle gently into its home. Curtis said goodbye and was free, and Daffodil knew he was gone, that she'd saved him. After all of the loss over the years, the many perceived triumphs and failures, the happiness she felt in her final Earthly moment was exquisite.

I'll give you one guess what the picture on the puzzle was.

Daffodil stared at the tree she watched Darius die protecting so many years ago. The one he was now a part of. The one her friend and protector Thomas Bankshot Jones had earned retirement on. The one Curtis was off to save. Daffodil shut her eyes and said a few closing words to Bob. Her work here was done.

I told you before time doesn't work like we perceive, though I could be incorrect. Maybe it does work as we perceive but simply can't account for jumping around multiple dimensions and alternate planes of existence. Or maybe time is just another one of reality's conventions that is absolutely irrelevant when dealing with the intricacies of Bob. However this all works, when Curtis Gout was freed from his prison in the old-lady Daffodil's jigsaw puzzle, Timmy was still on Euphoratopadopia chopping away at Kyle, the Tree of Souls.

Timmy was exhausted but his work was almost finished. Although the tree still stood, balanced by its own weight, the immortal symbol of knowledge, love, and wisdom throughout the universe was a few strikes away from being toppled. If not for Kyle's enormity,

Timmy would have already sent the tree crashing, and though in a severely weakened state, the tree still held more power than the monster. More than could ever be imagined.

Even Timmy, the scourge of the cosmos, succumbed to the beauty of Kyle and its world. Euphoratopadopia had healed Timmy's wounds and infected him with its charms. The monster had been chopping for a very, very long while. When he tired, Timmy would relax to enjoy the splendidness of his work. There was a part of him, an extremely far away, deeply buried emotion, which had purposefully slowed his work to avoid finishing his task. The aftermath of his impending victory was a mystery. His current mission was well known to him, and well to his liking.

A wistful breeze announced the arrival of Curtis Gout and his army. Remember all those kids Bobby had been running around the universe saving? The sound of their joyful war cries travelled with the wind. Timmy stopped in mid-swing of his anatomical ax and stood straight with a hmph. He returned his hands to their normal shape and used them to shade the sunlight from his eyes as he squinted into the distance. The monster first saw Curtis emerge atop the same hill he once topped himself, on his own final march towards destiny.

As Curtis' full shape came into view, so too did the forms of numerous other creatures. There were thousands of them triumphantly marching behind Curtis Gout, an army of cosmic innocence, though one might argue that having survived the destruction of their entire planets, civilizations, and species, their childlike innocence might have been lost. But, whomever attempted that argument would, in this instance, be incorrect, as they were all still children, now brothers and sisters (and whatever you call asexual siblings) of the same family. A hodgepodge of a family, the melted pot of survival, and existence's last ditched hope for redemption.

Timmy knew they were there for battle and decided to change shapes into something really scary to frighten the children away. Instead, he became a gigantic stuffed animal. The monster was a Pot Belly Teddy Bear as big as a house. Once transformed, Timmy sat thoroughly confused. *Was this what I meant to be?* he thought, but his insolent brain did not respond. This was the touch of Kyle, the effect of a monster having spent too much time in the light.

The children ran at Timmy, all smiles and laughter. They dove on him and began to tickle him giddily, climbing all over him. The monster changed shapes again, and this time became a giant puppy. No matter what evil, horrible, disgusting form he considered, Timmy continued to change shapes into adorable cuddly things that children love. But, whether evil be cute or evil be ugly, it's still evil. I won't sugar coat this, many children died that day.

Timmy managed to fight back in spite of the odds stacked against him. Although his evil was heavily tickled, many a giggling tiny soldier felt his wrath. Still, the assault was too much to bear. I don't know if it was overexposure to all the positivity he'd been surrounded by, or not being able to overpower the united thoughtfulness of the kids, but the monster succumbed to the sweet pain of their tickle. His resistance became half-hearted, as if he was fighting back because he knew he was supposed to, not because he really wanted to win. In the end, Timmy let go of the monster he was and laughed himself to death.

Okay, he didn't actually laugh to death but he did completely exhaust himself with the giggles. Like a child runs in circles that last fifteen minutes before bedtime, resisting their body's call for imme-diate rest before passing out in a parent's arms mid but-I-don't-want-to-go-to-sleep spasm, so too did the monster succumb to the need for immediate rest. The children backed away as Timmy settled down next to the tree and fell asleep. Then Curtis Gout walked over and cut Timmy's twisted, rotten, punk-ass heart out.

Then he ate it!

I'm just kidding. Curtis actually buried the heart under a large root near the base of the tree. Then he chopped off Timmy's head out of spite. Bob was pretty upset with him later for doing that in front of the kids.

"C'mon Bob, they already seen me cut the thing's heart out," Curtis would say, right before apologizing. Bob would not have to explain to Curtis that cutting out Timmy's heart was as unnecessary as chopping off the monster's head. Curtis already knew.

Timmy had actually died from the overwhelming positive ener-gy of the children. I suppose they killed him with kindness, so to speak. The monster could not resist their joy, nor their innocence, and when his darkness was lost there was nothing left of him. In fact, only one season passed before the soil of Euphoratopadopia claimed the rest of Timmy's body. I don't really know if the creature had a soul. Who knows if it did, or if it did, what happened to that soul when the monster died. I suppose Bob might. Me, I don't even understand how come a cosmic being's "remains" were represented by a physical body Curtis Gout was able to mutilate. All I know for certain is that Timmy was gone and my friend Kyle, the Tree of Souls, survived. Eventually he made a full recovery.

Universe saved. Hooray.

Once Timmy was defeated, Curtis took the children who survived back through the door into Daffodil's brain. Go figure, there were exactly as many children as there were other Daffodils. The motherless children and childrenless mothers were paired-up for motherhood and childhood, and each was sent through a different door. Bob doth work in mysterious ways.

You may find this odd considering the other versions of our Daffodil didn't have bodies. They were only personalities. Our Daffodil only had one body. I understand. How did a bunch of mentally projected personalities walk through dimensional gateways and manage to raise kids in the physical world? I know, this seems incongruous but somehow the transference worked.

Oh, right, the answer's in the question. Multiple dimensions. The other versions of our Daffodil's personality had taken over alternate physical versions of Daffodils on different plains of existence. That's what the deal was. Has to be the answer.

But what happened to the personalities that had already been in control of those bodies? Where did they go? Both are good questions.

Vegetables? You're damn right. That makes perfect sense. Every planet would have vegetables, and who said the bodies had to be alternate physical versions of Daffodils for our alternate mental versions of Daffodil to live in? No one, that's who. Using vegetables makes perfect sense, and there's no denying that braindead bodies are all over the place in this universe.

So that's the answer, right Bob? Daffodil's others were stuck inside empty bodies that weren't ready to kick the bucket but had lost their soul? Oh well, dear friend and reader, we may never know. Remember when I said that when you're dealing with the inner workings of the universe, sometimes you just have to let shit go? One way or another all the children had mothers, all the mothers had new bodies, and my Daffodil was finally whole. At least for a while.

Meanwhile, Curtis went back to the filling station. His brother was gone, maybe only for the time being. We still aren't certain exactly what happened to Bobby, but either way he was lost, which saddened Curtis. His old soul needed rest. Even though he'd been trapped in the jigsaw puzzle for a huge portion of our adventure he was still due for a long nap.

But of course, there's no rest for the wicked, or cosmic heroes. When Curtis got back to the filling station he discovered The King of Shar-Crypt-On, fully recovered from his coma and desperately searching for Mr. Brownstone.

"We have to find Jerry," said The King.

"Okay," Curtis answered. Man, he was super tired.

Daffodil and I, we moved on with life. As previously mentioned, we married, we had kids, and have continued our efforts to save the universe when called upon. In the end, someday she will die an old woman staring at a jigsaw puzzle. They still haven't decided what to do with me yet. But that's the future. For the moment, I'm still trapped here in this stupid room while my wife and children are somewhere out there waiting for me. Probably at home, asleep in their beds on the same night I was taken. That's usually how this shit works.

Daff, I'm coming, baby. I promise. All I have to do is wake-up one more time.

The End

EPILOGUE

There, I'm done. Bob? You there? I said I'm done. I'm finished. I wrote the book and told the truth. The universe is saved. Right?

Something isn't right. There were things I wanted to say, was supposed to say…

Atoms are made of three specific pieces. (For the sake of my forthcoming argument, let's just stick with protons, neutrons, and electrons. We'll leave the gluons, quarks and other sub-atomic nonsense out of this.) People seem to fall into three categories as well. Since we humans believe life revolves around us, doesn't it make sense that as a species, the human race would be made up of positive, negative, and neutral components, just like our fundamental building block, the tiny sexy atom?

A human can be born negative, which sucks, but at least when you're born negative it's not your fault. If nothing makes you happy then at least you know nothing makes you happy and you can settle into a grumpy life. This may be a terribly frustrating existence for that particular person, but for the rest of us it's an easy call:

"Look at that poor sonofabitch."

"Yeah, the universe really shit on him."

Then there's all those happy go lucky motherfuckers. Honestly, I think being born positive is almost as lame as being born negative. Constantly seeing the silver lining in the workings of the world may take a little more energy than negativity, but not much since it's merely how you were created. In fact, to the casual observer, innate positivity may seem disingenuous. Happy almost all the time? At peace in this world of madness and pain? Fuck you and your giant shiny truck.

Okay, shiny trucks and grumpy fucks accounted for, what about the rest of us? The rest of us are the neutrons, born neutral in a polarized universe. Empty vessels to be filled with innocence compromising data. We have to constantly choose, constantly fight between happy or sad, and that's exhausting. Fighting a never ending battle of conflicting emotions requires a lot of energy. I think the greater percentage of self-aware beings are born neutral, but I can't figure out why. How counter productive is that? A never ending cosmic tug of war between good and evil, positive and negative, and all of us neutral fuckers are the rope? Existence is confusing, simply baffling, often loving and often hateful. A formless jigsaw puzzle whose pieces span infinity, hiding from mixed metaphors. I'm tired. Universe be damned.

I wish I could just go to sleep and wake up at home (that was the plan). I wish I could tell you that none of this was true. This whole tale was purely my imaginings because I'm lonely, trapped here in this stupid room. I wish I could tell you that life was really fair, and in the long run makes complete sense, and eventually we get to know what "It" is all about. Unfortunately, I cannot, and even if I did, life would come along and pull the rug out from underneath that notion in short order. Otherwise, I wouldn't be trapped here in this cynical little room. Yes, I wish I could tell you that none of this was true, but it is. Every single bit. Especially the poorly written stuff.

All true. Except the stuff about me and Bob. That's all lies and conjecture, I think. I'm pretty sure those passages were my imaginings because I'm stuck here alone in this Bobforsaken room. I have no idea what he and I will talk about when we meet, unless those things I told you really happened and the only reason I'm now uncertain is because I'm currently off my rocker.

One way or the other, clearly I'm not certain there is an actual Bob, though I strongly consider the possibility we're all Bob. One unified organism with some form of unified conscious. One organism we're all part of, for which you may be a cancer or a cure. I prefer to think of myself as a freckle right behind her left ear. A tiny speck of imperfection waiting to be discovered by a meticulous lover.

You may find this shocking, but despite all I've been shown by the universe I have no idea what will happen when we die. Apparently the possibilities are endless. I'm gonna have to die if I want to find out what happens to me, and even then I won't know for sure 'cause I might just wake up and not remember anything. I could wind up in a frog, or the conscious of a star, or I could just be dead.

At least I know my wife will peacefully die of old age someday. If things stay the same as they are now, that is. Of course, things won't stay the same because they always change, but Daffodil still has a chance. I think. Dammit.

Non-sequitur: What if Bob really was a physical being and was the last of her kind, a species that evolved from humans, and she reinvented us so she could bring her people back? Maybe we're supposed to obliterate each other. Maybe that's how Bob's species was made in the first place. Each Bob is the end result of the destruction of an entire species. That's a plan I could believe, if only because humans appear to have the "obliterate each other" portion moving forward at a healthy pace.

Perhaps it all makes sense. Perhaps there is a design that is part of a plan and every choice we make moves us in the direction we were already heading anyways, providing us the illusion of free will. Maybe, just maybe, oh perhaps, just perhaps, Bob is real. Maybe my imaginings aren't really just imaginings. Maybe they are her words because she inspired me to write them. Maybe I should start a religion. Perhaps I, yes I, am an instrument of her progressive revelation. I doubt it, though I would not be surprised at all if you were.

If I did start a religion, I think I would go with three tenets, something along the lines of: Perhaps there is peace of mind in goodness. Perhaps there is enough food on this planet for everyone to have a meal. Perhaps we could make nonsense our faith and silliness our savior.

Nah… Would never work when we're already surrounded by religions and philosophies and economies. Surrounded by world leaders and murderers and athletes. Causes and jobs and hobbies and people, so many fucking people. The lists go on and on. Society is a merciless auctioneer, forcibly selling us worthless bullshit in exchange for our time, our thoughts, and in effect our very souls. You don't even have to believe in a soul to get the point. But, of all people, Bret Michaels and Poison may have said it best with these words from their greatest song: "…I didn't know now, the things I didn't know then. And give me something to believe in. Anything Bobdammit. Anything at all." (Those last two lines got cut in the studio.)

The point is that in the middle of all this insanity there is this entity out there, this theory, this physical presence, this completely existential thought, this nothing at all that doesn't exist, this embodiment of anything you want her to be, which, I repeat, includes nothing at all, that we all choose for ourselves. She's something and or nothing at the same time, I call her Bob, and I'm telling you, she just wants us to be kind to one another. Even if Bob isn't real, she's still real. Whether we like it or not, everybody has a Bob. Including evil, whose unfortunate negative birthright completely misses the point of existence: Be kind, motherfuckers. Be kind.

So, there's my naked moral to the story, laid bare in a few simple words, yet here I am, still trapped in this absurd little room. Why? All the clocks are gone. All my recording equipment is gone. The sand has sifted and the hourglass has disappeared. The story's told, the message illuminated, but I'm still here. Just me and four soft, white, padded fucking walls. Why? I may be a fool, but I'm not crazy, and this room is for people our world labels insane.

I'm not crazy I tell you, the universe is. You hear me Bob? I know you do. I did my job. I'm. Not. Crazy. I'm just tired. I'm tired and I can't sleep, and if I can't fall asleep, I can't go home. Let me sleep, Bob. Please? May I rest?

I give sleep another try. Eyes closed. Heartrate slowed. Conscious cleared. I wonder if those two dudes are still playing *Mike Tyson's Punch-Out*...

MISSION ASSIGNMENT: 514
SOUL TRANSMISSION: OMEGA-1
ACTIVE UNIT: 257-A
RECORDING TECHNICIAN: AO41

Wow, I did not see that coming. Nor this: I think I'm still in love. Highly unusual. I wonder if I know the soul in that young man, if we've met before. Truant Memphis. Kind of a dumb name.

Still, I feel a little bad for the kid. I wish he knew everything was going to be okay. That things are going to be different now. Speaking of which, my full report will have to wait. I've only logged on to tell you I will not be logging on for some time. There are stories to be told and work to be done, and I have to figure out how to get Truant back home to me before he loses the rest of his mind. Despite my apparent return to interdimensional stasis, Mission Assignment 514 appears to remain active. Omega-2 report will follow at an undetermined time.

How can I be here, yet somewhere still be alive on Earth, waiting for Truant to return to me? How can I be here, yet watching thousands of different versions of myself raise thousands of interstellar orphans? How can I be a free spirit of the cosmos helping Truant find his way back to my Earthly body again? I don't know, but I've always wondered what the -A in my name stood for. Apparently, my paradigm has shifted. Praise Bob.

Perhaps I'm not the only one. Chaos by design, paradox, that's Bob's deal. If you don't like it, dear Recording Technician, file a complaint. Mark up my file with red ink. Better yet, find Bob and request an interview. In the meantime, I'm going to help Curtis and The King find Mr. Brownstone, and figure out why Truant wasn't sent home, and we will all most likely save the universe a few more times.

That stated, I do have one more item for your current record and subsequent report. Upon returning to the Soul Closet, many have asked me what I said to Bob at the very end, when my physical body on Earth was giving out and I thought true death was waiting for me. The Last Words are common curiosity amongst those of us rotating across the stage of this grand theatre. As you may well know, once the present life has flashed before your mind's eyes, the convergence begins. All of your lives come flooding back to you, which can be confusing, enlightening, disheartening, glorious, any number of countless emotions. In this instance, I include this in my report due to its historical and legal relevance. I'll tell you what I told my compatriots in the Closet, and what I will continue to state on record for all of my eternity. At the very end, with my dying breath on Earth, I said, "Bob, Rohm-Bridicata was not my fault."

END TRANSMISSION

Truant Memphis is the creation of an egocentric yet wildly insecure Kentuckian desperately in search of peace or a buzz (immortality wouldn't be so bad either). The author has two previous titles available, *Littlethumb Sneezed* and *Post Oh!pocalypto Poppycock*. Both are certain to leave you at least mildly entertained, but if I did my job well, upon reading either one you might suddenly find yourself very comfortable with chaos. You can find links to purchase those and enjoy more of Truant's nonsense at www.truantmemphis.com. I hope you enjoyed my story. Be kind, motherfuckers. Be kind.